# Carby's Fate

# Carby's Fate

*Thomas J. Rice*

ISBN: 0986221619
ISBN 13: 9780986221613
Library of Congress Control Number: 2015905403
Barrow River Press, Andover, MA

Praise for **Carby's Fate**

"In *Carby's Fate*, Thomas Rice has fashioned a small masterpiece of Irish Literature. By turns compellingly dramatic and psychologically astute, Rice's story is ever engaging and moving, delivering in its final moment a surprising and satisfying fulfillment of promise."

Wayne Johnson, *New York Times* Notable Book and Pulitzer Prize nominated author of *Don't Think Twice* and seven other books.

"With characters so vivid you'll think you're sitting in the pub drinking a pint of Guinness with them, *Carby's Fate* weaves a tale of suspense, surprise and emancipation. Superb storyteller Thomas Rice brings to life an Irish village embroiled in a deep-rooted and emotional controversy, pulling the reader squarely into the fray and not letting go till it's over."

Carol Ann Wilson, award-winning author of *Still Point of the Turning World: The Life of Gia-fu Feng.*

Thomas J. Rice has done it again. Following on the success of his "Hard Truths," published in *The Best American Mystery Stories of 2012*, he once again lets us in on the hidden stories and prejudices of yet another remote Irish village, complete with... eccentric characters... terrible choices and.. decisions allow us to see into their true natures. You'll never forget Carby, the ... central character.

Margaret E. Ward, American journalist and broadcaster based in Dublin, Ireland.

For Annie

# Carby's Fate

A WET AND BLUSTERY OCTOBER evening in Rathdangan, and P.J. Finnegan's, the only pub in this south Leinster village, was beginning to buzz with the regulars. The local band was tuning up for the Wednesday night ballad session, and the first couple of pints were beginning to soothe the raw edges of the bone-chilling day.

Five kilometers away, a sleek Mercedes-Benz sedan with a German vanity plate marked "MD" (Managing Director) pulled in at a bus stop, about a kilometer south of a busy crossroads. In spite of the swirling rain, all four windows of the sedan were wide open. The signpost held three black and white markers: "Dublin 60 km; Kilkenny 14km; Rathdangan 5 km."

The driver was a stylishly dressed businessman in his late fifties. He sported an expensive Swiss watch and gold cuff links. He turned to the passenger, smiled stiffly, said something in parting, and looked impatiently at his watch. The passenger, a small, pockmarked man who'd been crouched down in the passenger seat, sat up, looked about, and quickly shook hands with the driver. They exchanged no further comments; the passenger stepped into the rainy night, and the driver quickly closed the windows before turning the Mercedes north on the Dublin Road.

The passenger watched it drive out of sight, then glanced furtively about before pulling a rusted Raleigh bike from behind a hawthorn hedge. He rode the bike up to the intersection and stopped, cars drenching his trousers as they swished by in the gathering dusk. He looked at the drowning moon, then walked the bike across the new, six-lane M5. He nervously checked the traffic, remounted, and pedaled doggedly down the narrow road marked "Rathdangan."

Pulling pints behind the bar, I noticed Carby Bolger still missing from his solitary spot near the back door. One thing you could always count on: Carby would be the last man in, regardless of how staggered or late the others might be. But even by last man standards, tonight he was pushing the limit by almost two hours.

Paddy Crotty, who was usually too busy speechifying to notice anything else, now spoke for the rest of us. "I wonder what's holdin' Carby up tonight," he bellowed. "Maybe something happened to the da. It's not like that man to miss post time." Everyone laughed, not because it was funny, but because Crotty was our local representative to parliament ("Dail Eireann") and fancied himself a standup comedian, so we all obliged. No harm in it: like most things in Rathdangan, we did it out of habit.

Shortly after nine o'clock—the band having finished their first set—Carby ambled through the door, dripping wet, but dressed in his Sunday best on a Wednesday night. No one dared ask him where he'd been or why the suit and tie. That would have to wait. Carby was not a man to share his personal life and, truth to tell, we all knew it by heart anyway. Still, we were curious about the egregiously late arrival and the dress up. I'd ferret it out later.

Bartenders are supposed to know their regulars, and I knew a lot about Carby Bolger, going way back. There was something about him that always repelled people. Me, too—I just hid it a bit better than most. He'd come into Finnegan's and order two pints of Guinness at once, nursing them till closing time in his cubby, always alone. I'd serve him as I did everyone, with the usual "Howyagoin' on Carby?" But all I ever got was a curt, "Awright." I took it as, "Feck off, and leave me ta hell alone!" I don't know why I even bothered with the nasty little bollix.

He was christened Patrick Edward Bolger—after Packie, his paternal grandfather. The family always called him Patrick, but everyone else called him Carby—a nickname with a cruel origin. It started as a fourth grade taunt about the oozing carbuncles disfiguring his small, pale face. The nickname stuck, as did the pockmarks and red scars that gave him the look of someone who'd been shot in the face at close range.

Yet, for all his weirdness, there was nothing about Carby's demeanor or track record that would lead us to predict that he was destined to put Rathdangan on the map: a household name across Ireland, a familiar name in Europe, and even in America. He'd sit there alone, smoking cheap Woodbines in his dark cubby, greasy cap pulled down over his beady little darting eyes.

He had a strong body odor; most of the regulars did—but at least they smelled organic, like natural farmers. Carby's odor was different, especially of late. He had this stench that went beyond the usual dried sweat, tobacco, turf, and cow shite; it was something chemical, sulfuric, and nauseating, a bit like rotten eggs. The locals could always tell he was in the pub before they saw him lurking in the corner, long before they heard the hacking cigarette cough fracturing the air in loud spasms, some lasting several minutes.

With Carby such an odd ball, one would expect to find some insight close at hand in the Bolger family. But such a line of inquiry would be perplexing. His parents, Andy and Mary, were the salt-of-the-earth: widely respected, loyal friends, and generous neighbors. Andy, Carby's da, had been the oldest of five, a natural athlete with blonde hair and an open, boyish smile. He'd been a legendary midfielder for the Kilkenny Senior Hurling

Team, playing till his late-forties. He'd also been a gifted fiddler, started his own band, and had held a lasting passion for Irish step dancing. Being the oldest son, Andy had inherited the farm, worked hard, and had done his best to care for his aging parents and do right by the younger ones before bringing Mary, his bride, into the home place.

Mary was a Joyce from nearby Gowran, her family highly respected, well-heeled farmers. They cultivated over 100 acres of rich, arable land—flat as a ballroom floor, running parallel to the storied Barrow River. Mary was a classic Irish beauty, brunette ringlets springing from under her signature red beret. She had deep-set blue eyes that lit up the room, and long, shapely legs that few men ever forgot. She'd also been known for her elegant step dancing and sweet soprano voice.

She'd graduated from the prestigious Convent School in Goresbridge, won a music scholarship to the National University (UCC) in Cork, and had been poised to escape farming, a first in the Joyce family. That was before she met Andy Bolger at a dance one Sunday night in Kilkenny, the same night he'd starred for the Rathdangan Rovers hurling team in the county championship. He'd been the man of the hour, and, like the rest of the county, Mary was smitten. It was goodbye university, hello hardscrabble 40 acres in Rathdangan.

There would be no dowry for a place like that, not from a beauty "marrying down."

Andy and Mary had four children, one boy and three girls, in rapid succession. First came Patrick, in October, 1955; then Molly, the perfect "Irish twin"—eleven months later; next were the actual twins, Hannah and Lizzie, just a year later, in September '57.

Patrick, though a robust baby at birth—weighing over 10 pounds—was colicky from the start, fussy with feeding, failing to thrive. He withered before Mary's eyes, reminding her of starving African children she'd seen on the cover of *National Geographic*. Dr. Breen, the local G.P., was little help, assuring Mary that he'd "grow out of it." Poor, suffering child, she reflected. He didn't even look like anyone in the family.

The baby's exotic appearance gave rise to salacious speculation on the genesis of his "foreign looks." He was small and swarthy, with jet black eyes close together, and wispy tufts of hair that only covered patches of his scrawny little head. As usual, the talk was all whispered behind the "squinting window"—the vicious rumor mill that never seemed to stop churning.

Perhaps the true explanation was less titillating: a mix-up in the maternity ward. Two famous cases had been documented at St. Luke's General after anxious parents became suspicious. Those cases were still dragging through the courts. But it was not in the Bolger's nature to be suspicious or to sue anyone. They loved their baby boy and accepted him as their own.

But if Patrick's presence was a mixed blessing, Molly's arrival brought the Bolgers a new lease on life. Like an emotional cavalry charging to the rescue, she was a joyous contrast to their first-born in every respect. She smiled the first time she opened her bright blue eyes, drank heartily from her mother's breast, slept through the night except for feeding, and seemed delighted to be in the world. Like Andy, her father, she was blonde, with her mother's curls, smile, and graceful beauty. There was no doubt about this girl's heritage. She was a perfect blend of Bolger and Joyce.

Shortly after, the twins followed suit, except they made a team effort in expressing the bloodlines—Hannah was a Joyce; Elizabeth a Bolger. From birth they both had a gift for comedy, seeming to have a routine worked out for every audience. Hannah had her mother's brunette coloring, long legs, and high cheekbones. Lizzie, like her da, was constantly in motion and captured all hearts with her precocious musicality and gap-toothed smile.

Who knows what growing up with such attractive and talented siblings does to a person like Carby? He and I were in the same class at Rathdangan National School, starting in '61. We all knew that, being the oldest male, he'd inherit the family farm, while landless lads, like most of us, had little alternative but to emigrate.

Still, I didn't envy him one bit—even for a minute. I actually felt sorry for him; he never had a single friend and was like a punching bag for every bully in the schoolyard. He didn't even try to defend himself; he'd just put his arms over his face and take the abuse. Never cried either; it was weird to watch, which the rest of us did without lifting a finger in his defense. We just saw it as first-rate entertainment.

As expected, Carby failed every subject, year after year. It wasn't that he was slow—just uninterested. And stubborn as a mule. Our teacher up to fourth grade, Mrs. Donovan, was an anomaly for her time—patient and kind, dedicated to our learning. We took advantage of her good nature, of course, but Carby went beyond the pale at every turn. Each time she asked him a question, he'd come at her as though she was invading his privacy, with: "How do I know whin we got our independence?" Or, "There's no use in axin' me. I have no interest in dat kinda auld shite."

Once, after Carby had erupted in a classic outburst, she ordered him to go stand in the hallway, "...Till you learn some manners." He just glared at her and muttered, "Feck off. Go stand dere yerself!" If she'd reported him to Mr. Ryan, the Master, he'd have beaten Carby within an inch of his life. But Mrs. Donovan kept her cool. She reached down and grabbed his arm to pull him out of his wooden desk. But Carby dug in, refusing to budge, so she had to drag him, still glued to his desk, all the way across the room and into the hallway. I can still see the marks and hear the metal legs screeching on the hardwood floor, like the amplified sound of fingernails scraping on a blackboard. Coming back in the room, with Carby parked in the hallway, Mrs. Donovan slammed the door so hard it shook the whole building. We trembled and giggled at the same time.

Secretly, we loved it when Carby went off on Mrs. Donovan. No one else would dare push their luck, but he seemed to enjoy the tussle, smiling his little half-smile—as if at his own orneriness. We'd all laugh and try to imitate him on the playground, with, "Do Carby! Do Carby!" requests coming at Pete Dunphy, a gifted mimic. All this within earshot of Carby, who just sat there, chewing his fingernails, dark eyes smoldering, glaring at us from his perch on the dilapidated stone wall dividing the schoolyard.

Carby quit Rathdangan National on his fourteenth birthday, as soon as the law would allow. I remember it well, since we spent that entire week doing Carby imitations. It was great craic. Then I promptly forgot about him, for almost two decades.

I went on to secondary school in St. Molins and graduated with A levels before joining the emigration parade to New York. It was hard to leave Rathdangan. I'd been born with an athletic gift, which I'd poured into hurling—our national passion, especially in Kilkenny—and starred on every team I'd played for since I was 7. I made the county minors at 16, the seniors at 18—the youngest player in their storied history—and we'd won three All-Ireland Championships ('72, '74, & '75) before I emigrated, and they flew me home for three more ('79, '82, & '83) while I was in New York. I was high scorer in four out of the six, so I had the kind of local cachet that many had parlayed into successful political careers at home. But none of that mattered in 1970s Ireland—we were just another third-world country, an isolated island in the rainy North Atlantic. And hurling trophies didn't pay the rent or fill the shopping bags at the grocery store.

So, with a heavy heart and just a few extra quid after I paid for the ferry ticket, I left Rathdangan in 1975; there was no real choice. Those were the bad old days of mass emigration from Ireland. I lost track of Carby completely until I came home eleven years later—in 1986, right after my Uncle Tommy bought P.J. Finnegan's, the central (only) attraction of Rathdangan village. After 60 years of singlehandedly running the pub, Old Paddy Finnegan—a widower—wasn't up to it anymore, and his only son, Mick, had left for Australia after a fight with his da. Paddy never mentioned Mick again, and people soon stopped asking after him.

New York had been good to me. After two years patching it together with odd jobs, I'd scored again—this time a full scholarship to New York University (NYU) in Manhattan, after winning an essay competition sponsored by *The New Yorker* magazine. As luck would have it, there were no jobs for English majors in New York City in '82, the year I graduated, so I kept my bartending gig— the one that got me through college—at The Green Drake on 3rd Avenue, a gritty Irish pub where you could easily find trouble. When Uncle Tommy came up with this job offer at P.J. Finnegan's over Christmas holidays, I jumped at the chance to be home, where I belonged. I'd never wanted to leave in the first place, so I thought I'd died and gone to heaven.

I came home to a hero's welcome—the Kilkenny GAA (Gaelic Athletic Association) threw a homecoming parade and hosted a blowout party in my honor at the Kildara Arms. Still basking in the glow of six All-Ireland Championships in just over a decade, an historic first, I immediately picked up where I'd left off, this time as a player/coach, working for Nick Barry, my role model as an athlete and Kilkenny captain from the '50s.

Fortune was smiling on me now. Not only was Rathdangan my long-lost "bosom of Abraham," it was an ideal place to finish my first book, *Moon Over Mount Leinster* (historical fiction about Wolfe Tone's failed insurrection in 1798). It was also a good time to escape the urban jungle that New York City was rapidly becoming in the '80s.

My first night behind the bar at Finnegan's, who wanders in but Carby! He hadn't changed a bit: still short, skin draped carelessly over bones; same dark, darting eyes, as if he were being stalked by some ghostly predator.

I greeted him like a long-lost pal. "Carby, how the hell are ya?" I shouted with feigned delight. "Man! Oh, man! It's great to see ya!"

Fair play to him, he was having none of it. He glanced at the floor, offered a fishy handshake, then jerked his hand away quickly, as if I might claim it. Without a hint of meeting my eyes, he said, "Gimme two pints o' Guinness; I'll be over here by the back door," and shuffled away to his cubby. Later I learned that this was known as "Carby's stall," one not likely to be coveted by anyone else.

Catching up on the local gossip over the next few weeks, I learned that fate had dealt the Bolgers a terrible hand. First it was Andy, Carby's da. A lifelong pipe smoker, he'd been stricken with throat cancer—and had lost his vocal cords. A few years later, the cancer spread to his lungs, and he was confined to a wheelchair, wheezing, needing full-time nursing care. Molly, their oldest daughter, who'd risen to the top of the nursing profession in Dublin, then London, came to the rescue. A year later, Andy's wife, Mary, was diagnosed with pancreatic cancer and died within months.

The twins had emigrated to the U.S.—Hannah now practiced law in San Francisco; Lizzie, now Professor Elizabeth Bolger, taught history at Boston College. They came home for their mother's funeral, expressed their gratitude for Molly's sacrifice, then got on with their lives, leaving Molly to do the heavy lifting. Carby worked the farm in his own random fashion, seldom spoke to the neighbors, and was known to one and all as "odd"—a prickly, foul-smelling loner.

Though I kept it to myself, I'd always had a crush on Molly Bolger. Truth to tell, most of the lads in the village did. She was beautiful and elegantly turned out, but elusive as a fawn. Unlike the twins or other village girls, she never went to the *ceili* dances and never dated any of the locals. The "squintin' window" gossip mill had it that "Molly didn't like men," as if the choices she faced in Rathdangan exhausted the universe of eligibles.

One of the few times I ever spoke to her alone was the day she got a flat down the road from Finnegan's. She'd walked back to the pub for help, and I drove her the half mile in Uncle Tommy's car. I changed the tire on her little Morris Minor, and we chatted briefly and joked about my hurling addiction—still a player/coach—and long-standing ambition to write historical fiction.

After we ran out of chit-chat, I said, "Now don't be a stranger in Finnegan's, Molly. Stop in an' see us; I'll buy the first round. I promise we won't bite." She'd smiled, shook my hand warmly with both of hers, and I was a goner. I can still see that yellow dress and smell the exotic perfume—just like her, elegant and memorable. But I didn't have the brass to ask her for a date; never understood how some guys just up and did that.

If I'd asked her out that day, things might have turned out differently for Carby and the Bolgers. Molly never did come back for that drink, and I never got up the nerve to go find her. A few years later, though barely turned thirty, Molly fell victim to that deadly label for women who hadn't been claimed by some local dairy farmer who happened to be the oldest male in his family: she was deemed to be "on the shelf"—another spinster assigned to second-class citizenship in Rathdangan.

Independent of beauty or intelligence, a single woman's place in Rathdangan was taking care of her parents in their old age; bachelor uncles or brothers came with the territory. This was assumed as the natural order of things. The arrangement was frozen as a fossil in the culture: ordained by God, modeled by the Blessed Virgin, and enforced by the priesthood and self-appointed soothsayers.

That was before Molly Bolger took a wrecking ball to the natural order, reminding the entire village that perhaps she had a lot more in common with Carby (our familiar deviant) than any of us suspected. One Sunday morning in late June of '87, she walked into Mass—all the way up front to the family pew—sporting a stylish maternity dress, unmistakably pregnant. The convulsive village reflex, usually reserved for Carby's exploits, was voiced repeatedly by Peggy Carroll, chief moralizer and "squinting window" gabster: "The nerve of her; bad enough that she disgraces her entire family, but she has to parade it before the *entire parish*." I could never figure out which was Molly's greatest sin—getting pregnant without a wedding ring, or not being ashamed of it.

Instantly a social pariah, just like her brother, Molly resolutely ignored the disapproving stares and the "squinting window" tongues. She simply went about the business of caring for the men in her family—Andy and Carby—running the farmhouse, and keeping everything on an even keel—right up to the day she gave birth.

The baby—a lusty boy—was born at St. Luke's Hospital in Kilkenny, December 23, 1987. He weighed 9 pounds, 8 ounces, had a voracious appetite, Bolger-blue eyes, and lungs that could wake the dead. He was christened Andrew Noel Bolger (he'd be known as Noel). Over the objections of the doctor and staff, Molly checked herself out of St. Luke's on Christmas morning and took a taxi home so that she could cook dinner for the family.

Delighted with his new grandson, Andy suddenly appeared to be in remission, charging about with his famous smile and a new spring in his step. It was as though this baby—named after his grandfather—with his busy fingers, piston legs, and powerful lungs, came endowed with secret healing powers that had eluded some of the best oncologists in Ireland.

But a few weeks later, the cancer was back, playing the predator's game, before pouncing on what was left of Andy's esophagus and lungs. He gamely refused a fourth operation, giving up the ghost on the night of February 10th, 1988. He'd known his grandson less than two months, just long enough to fall rapturously in love with the charismatic infant.

The wake was a lugubrious affair hosted by a swirling wind that moaned through the hawthorns as it prowled the dark winter landscape. After a perfunctory visit to pay their respects to the "dearly departed," the men withdrew to the kitchen, huddled in small groups, drank Guinness, and told tales of events that mostly never happened. The women stayed in the parlor, consoling Molly, who looked pale and red-eyed from sleepless grief.

Carby, as usual, sat silently by the AGA stove, looking and smelling his distinctive self. He showed no emotion as people shook his limp hand and muttered the obligatory, "Sorry for yer trouble, Carby." He said nothing, making no eye contact. He still wore his tattered Harris tweed, and stared at the ground, head in hands—his trademark posture.

The funeral was the biggest in Rathdangan history, with over 300 cars parked like sardines, all the way back to St. Molin's Cross—over a mile from the graveyard. In the postmortem at Finnegan's, it was said without irony that Andy's funeral was the "most popular" to ever grace the chapel in Rathdangan.

The night of the funeral, Carby was the last one to leave Finnegan's, after nursing his customary two pints in his cubby. Even in his hour of grief, not a single soul reached out with compassion or generosity. Not that we lacked either. It was just that no one dared risk the rebuff, or worse—ridicule—that was likely to follow any such gesture.

That was all before the dispute and Judge Flanagan's rulings would challenge another cornerstone of the natural order in Rathdangan, this time in a way that no one in the village—certainly not I—could ever have imagined.

The trouble began the day after Andy's funeral. Oblivious to his father's will and eager to establish his new standing as man-of-the-house, Carby biked into town and made an appointment with Bill Brady, Rathdangan's sole solicitor, to "administer" for the farm. Brady's chatty secretary, Siobhan Murphy, found an opening for one week later—Tuesday, at 2 p.m. Though Andy had left a will, it was the custom for the firstborn male to inherit the entire estate, leaving it up to him to deal with other siblings as he saw fit. This custom was unquestioned in rural Ireland—indeed throughout Europe, since medieval times—so it was simply a matter of drawing up the papers and paying a small fee to transfer title and establish full ownership.

A week later, Andy's solicitor, Phillip O'Shea—known locally as Phil Shea, managing partner in Murphy, O'Shea, & Finnegan, Barristers-at-Law, a prestigious law firm in Enniscorthy, County Wexford—served notice that this feudal arrangement had been dismantled by his deceased client, Andy Bolger, as he read the will to Carby and Molly, having invited them to his office some twenty miles from Rathdangan. Andrew Noel Bolger, the new grandson—NOT Carby—would inherit the home place, and Molly would be the legal guardian and executor of her father's will. Patrick was expressly cut out of his father's last will and testament.

Though an innocent bystander to Andy's decision, Molly was a ready-made target for the howls of indignation that erupted when the word got out. Looking back, I'm still amazed at how instantly united the entire community became in its campaign of ridicule and defiance, as if it had been rehearsing for such an eventuality for decades. I should have realized you don't need to rehearse what you practice every day as second nature.

Matt Murphy was first to spread the news in Finnegan's, having heard it from his chatterbox sister Siobhan, Bill Brady's secretary. From there, the drama unfolded like an Italian opera. Murphy speculated that the culprit must have been Hannah, the twin sister, the attorney who had visited from San Francisco. As he told the story—as the gospel truth—Hannah had browbeat her ailing father, Andy, to "do what Mammy would have wanted you to do" for Molly and her son, Noel. The upshot: inverting the age-old custom, leaving it up to *Molly* to decide Carby's fate.

Whatever led Andy Bolger to make such a drastic move, he never explained his thinking to anyone—not to Carby, not to Molly, not even to his solicitor, Phil Shea. It still makes no sense to me how a kind, thoughtful man—as we all knew Andy Bolger to be—could fail to anticipate what a devastating blow his decision would be to Carby, his only son. I will never believe that he didn't care; that was simply not his nature.

No one would ever know for sure, but (years later) Molly told me it might have been inspired by Carby's indifference—bordering on abuse—to his parents' needs for years while they had still been in good health. "He'd even forget the little things they asked for when he went to the village," she said wistfully. "Daddy's Twist tobacco, and Mammy's *Ireland's Own* (serial stories)—little creature comforts. In the end, I couldn't stand by and watch it. I just quit my post in London and came home. He really left me no choice."

According to the Finnegan buzz, Carby didn't take the news well. "Over me fucken dead body," was his reported response, after Phil Shea read them the will in his office. He had escalated from there, ranting, threatening violence, and brandishing a pitchfork at Molly after they got home. He spewed forth a rich array of epithets, including "fucken whure." And then, the *pièce de résistance*: "Now get ye an' yer little bastard off me land before I ram dis sprong up yer arse, ya goddamn slut."

Jack Dunphy, the mailman, overheard the hideous threat, so it was entirely credible, given Jack's reputation as a man of discretion. The story was otherwise embellished with creative riffs over the following weeks and months, building to an epic morality tale from random snippets of rumor, everyone speaking with the certainty of righteous eyewitnesses.

Molly, afraid for her baby's safety, if not her own, was shaken by her brother's behavior, which was simply beyond the pale. She was not surprised by his anger, of course—he had every right to be upset—but not to be this foul-mouthed, fork-wielding *beast*. So she simply packed her meager belongings—two suitcases and a hatbox—and moved to a small one-bedroom apartment in Goresbridge—a walkup over the hardware store on Parnell Street. It was the closest village down the Barrow. Next she called the family solicitor, Phil Shea, and told him what had just transpired.

After all, it was Phil who'd written their father's will; it was Phil who'd broken the news to them together; and it was Phil whom she trusted to advise her on her rights and the proper legal course of action that was now called for.

Phillip O'Shea was an anomaly among Irish barristers. He was born and raised in London by Irish parents, his father a successful surgeon who'd converted to Protestantism and become an ardent Anglophile, in love with all things British. While attending Trinity Law School, Phillip fell in love with all things Irish: its poetry, landscape, pubs, and people. He'd reclaimed his ancestral culture, and never left. Handsome, athletic, and popular with men and women—now in his late forties—Phil was seen as a highly eligible bachelor who liked to "play the field," and showed no inclination to marry and settle down.

The squinting window (gossip mill) had it that Phil might be Noel's father; others speculated it was a former lover Molly had known from her days in London. I didn't care who the father was. I just thought she got a raw deal: stuck with two ailing parents, a barren farm, and Carby.

Now this.

Ever since that flat tire, she'd been on my mind. I'd fantasized about ways to run into Molly again. Perhaps ask her for a date. But I'd never had any confidence around attractive women. And, as a practical matter, I couldn't even afford to take her out to a dance. Living on bartender's wages, I didn't own a car. I was borrowing Uncle Tommy's 20-year-old Austin any time I needed to get things for the pub. Who was I kidding? How could I expect to court a woman of Molly Bolger's class? And now that she had the farm, it only made things worse. I knew what the squinting window would say if I so much as asked her to the movies.

Whatever her relationship with Phil Shea, Molly hired him to represent her son's legal interests. And so it was that Phil drafted the dreaded "solicitor's letter" and had it delivered to Carby at the farm.

The essence of the letter was that Molly had rights and obligations as executor of the Bolger estate, and she was not going to be bullied out of them. What were these rights and obligations? She outlined her case to Phil, which he translated into obtuse legalese befitting a talented barrister. The final draft read as follows:

**Murphy, O'Shea & Finnegan**
**Barristers-at-law**
**45 Rosslare Road**
**Enniscorthy, Co. Wexford**

**February 21, 1988**
**Mr. Patrick E. Bolger**
**Rathdangan, Co. Carlow**

**Dear Mr. Bolger,**

**I have been asked to represent your sister, Ms. Molly Bolger, as executor of the family estate at Rathdangan, constituting approximately 40 acres of freehold land and dwellings, registered in the Townland of Drimoland under the absolute ownership of Andrew J. Bolger, titleholder to same since 1966. The land is subject to the provisions on subletting and subdivision specified in Sec. 12 of the Land Act of 1965, which specifies the vesting of interests in Section 45 of said Act in so far as said Provisions affect the same.**

To wit, we hereby wish to inform you that Andrew E. Bolger, sole owner of the afore-mentioned property, and "being of sound and disposing mind and memory and aware of the uncertainties of this mortal life," lodged and published his last will and testimony with my firm a month before his death on February 10, 1988. A copy of his will is enclosed, dated January 15, 1988. It leaves the entire estate at Rathdangan to his grandson, Andrew Noel Bolger, aged two months.

The will was witnessed and notarized in our office on January 30, 1987, at which time Mr. Bolger appointed his daughter, Mary (Molly) J. Bolger as executor of the Rathdangan estate with full powers of execution and discretion as to the timing of title transfer. The normal expectation for such a transfer to a minor descendant would be at age 18. But, we emphasize, it is strictly at the discretion of the executor. Equally, she is empowered to make any settlement she considers appropriate with the remaining siblings, including Patrick Edward Bolger, Elizabeth Marie Bolger, and Hannah May Harrington (née Bolger).

We understand that you intend to dispute this will and that you have threatened violence toward the heir and his mother. By way of this letter, we inform you that any further threats will be reported to the garda and you will answer for them. For now, you stand warned and cautioned.

In the meantime, your sister has taken the extraordinarily generous position of extending you forgiveness for these threats, and is prepared to make an offer, not based on the arbitrary custom of primogeniture or the last will and testament of her father. Rather, she wishes to be fair and equitable and is prepared to award you half the estate in recognition of your labors over the years and out of respect for the tradition that led you to a reasonable expectation of full inheritance.

For the record, this principle of equity squarely challenges the premise of primogeniture, which was overturned in Finnegan v. Crowley in 1954 and again in McGee v. Haughey in 1960. The court found for the plaintiff, a female sibling, in both cases, based on documented merit, not gender or birth order, as had been the ancient custom.

Following these legal precedents, both of which were appealed and upheld by the High Court, we put forth the following for your consideration:

Recognizing that the market value of the entire estate in its current condition is estimated at £100,000, my client is prepared to make the offer of a settlement for a modest £50,000, to be paid out by you over 10 years at the rate of £5,000 per year, plus accumulated interest (at current prime rate) on the balance of the principal. The full amount may be paid in one lump sum without penalty at any time before final payment is made. She offers these terms in order that you may keep the farm at Rathdangan intact and continue with your way of life undisturbed.

We trust you'll find these terms to be acceptable and generous under the circumstances. Your sister has no interest in claiming what is legally her son's property, since she considers that unfair to you. She only wishes for an amicable and fair settlement so that she and her son, on the one hand, and you, on the other, can both move on with unburdened, independent lives, and goodwill in the family.

**I look forward to hearing from you in the affirmative after you've considered this generous offer, at which time we can discuss legal transfer, issues of timing, and practicalities of payments.**

**Sincerely yours,**

––––––––––––––––––
**Phillip E. O'Shea, B.C.L.**
**Managing Partner**

The letter was delivered by courier in a large, sealed envelope. Phil didn't want to leave any doubt in Carby's mind that reality had set in, and while it was not what Carby might want, it would undoubtedly be more than he expected. Mick Dolan, the courier, a bull-necked former rugby forward from Cardiff, served the papers on Carby. He pulled right up to the farmhouse door in his yellow Land Rover, rapped loudly, and waited while Carby signed for the delivery.

An hour later, Carby stood ringing the doorbell of a brass-plated Victorian door at the top of the village. It read: "William F. Brady III, Solicitor at Law." Cap in hand, Carby bowed his head and inquired in a barely audible whisper, "Can I come in? I have some bad news. I need yer advice an this wan." Bill Brady, the only solicitor in Rathdangan, glad for the break from drafting a will, was eager to hear what Carby wanted. "Sure, sure. Come in, Carby. What can I do for you?" Carby did not reply, just handed Brady the crisp letter.

Sitting behind his large, oak desk—a family heirloom—Brady lit his pipe, read the letter from Phil Shea, read it again, then a third time, as if he couldn't believe what he was seeing on the page. Looking up, finally, he tried to meet Carby's darting eyes with an expression of concern, still holding the stiff, two-page letter.

"Well, Carby, this must have been shocking news to you; it is to me, quite frankly. If I read this correctly, your sister's boy inherited the farm with her as the the executor till he grows up. Meanwhile, she has complete say as to what happens; who gets what and so on... But you can look on the bright side: She's offering you half the farm for free, and the rest on reasonable terms... although she's not legally bound to do any of this. It could be worse, my friend. No point in looking a gift horse in the mouth, is what I say." Brady set the letter aside and waited for Carby's reaction.

"But she doesn't have a feckin' leg ta stand on," he shouted, as if Brady was deaf. "I own the farm an' dat's a fact. Da always said dat, even whin I was little... he'd say: 'Begob, son, you'll make a fine farmer someday whin ya take over an' yer auld da is pushin' up the daisies.'" For an instant, Carby choked up at the memory, then quickly collected himself, blushing and wiping his hand across his eyes.

"Besides, she hates da farm… she just wants ta grab it for dat little bastard o' hers… An' where am I gonna get 50,000 quid, for Chrissakes? Tis a fecking joke is what a tis. She's out ta bankrupt me! Dat's what she really wants; I know her game. I never trusted dat bitch for a minute, ever since she come home." As he spoke, he became angrier, punching the air and pacing the floor as he ranted on. "Who the feck does she t'ink she's kiddin? No way am I givin' her a single penny… she can go straight ta hell." Pacing nervously back and forth in Brady's large office, he rummaged feverishly in his coat pockets, fished out a pack of Woodbine cigarettes, and lit up, his tobacco-stained fingers shaking slightly.

Brady watched and listened intently, with a look of perfect neutrality. He waited for Carby to get it all out, then methodically relit his pipe, blew a whiff toward the window, and rendered his opinion in a slow, deliberate voice: "Carby, I understand how hard this must be, but I have to tell you that if this goes to court, you have no case. Your sister has all the cards, I'm afraid; she doesn't have to give you a penny if she doesn't want to. The custom of primogeniture is not a legal defense; it's been overturned dozens of times in courts across the country, and upheld time and again on appeal."

Carby lit another Woodbine directly off the barely-smoked first one, inhaled convulsively, and stared at the floor. Brady checked Carby's body language and decided to press on.

"I'd just be wasting your money to take this to court, especially in light of your sister's generous offer here. Your best bet is to negotiate the best deal you can— ask her to throw in the livestock and implements, say—and move on. Others may differ, but that's my professional opinion. I'd just hate to see you go broke trying to fight Molly in the courts and lose the whole farm to boot. Half a loaf is better than none; don't lose sight of that. She doesn't have to be this generous, you know. Go home and think about it." Brady's tone did not invite a rebuttal. He tapped the pipe against his hand, set it aside, and folded his hands in a gesture of finality.

Carby stared at him across the oak desk, dark eyes burning like coals. After several attempts to speak, he finally found his voice: "So… so dat's all ya hav' ta say? Dat's it? Yer tellin' me I hav' ta take dis lying down, like a dog dat's been kicked. Well let me tell ya something, Mister Brady, an' it's what I tauld dat bitch whin she first brought dis up: Over me fucken dead body! Dat's me answer to all a yez. Dey'll have to kill me ta take dat farm. I've worked for dis all me life, like me father before me, an' I'm not for just givin' it away to some fucken greedy trollop an' her bastard son."

Before Brady could get a word in, Carby stormed out, pulling the greasy cap tightly over his smoldering eyes. In the parking lot, still raging at Brady's counsel, he fired up his tractor and slammed it into gear, vowing this would be the last time he'd ever set foot in a solicitor's office.

As things turned out, it was a vow he would break before the month was out. I got it straight from the horse's mouth at Finnegan's—from none other than Matt Murphy, whose sister Siobhan had given him the insider's account. It seems that Phil Shea got tired of waiting for Carby to respond, and decided to call Bill Brady to find out if Carby had seen the light.

As Siobhan delighted in reporting, Phil got right to the point: "Phillip O'Shea here, Bill—How's that decision coming with Carby Bolger?"

Brady had immediately recognized the Oxford accent, was a bit taken aback, and had stalled for time to consider the ethics of his position. He thought of feigning ignorance, but there was no point. Everyone in the village knew of Carby's visit. He'd made sure of that with his repeated tirades at Finnegan's.

"Well, Phil, to be perfectly candid, I don't know. You see, I'm not representing Mr. Bolger in this matter. He came in with your letter sure enough, didn't like the opinion I offered, and stormed off. So I have nothing to report."

"I'm sorry to hear that, Bill," Shea had replied. "He'll never get a better deal, certainly not from Flanagan's bench in Kilkenny. He's murder on these Neanderthal types in family disputes, especially the ones who try to terrorize vulnerable women. He was raised by a single mum, you know... alcoholic da... usual profile..."

Brady just listened, aware that he was walking a fine ethical line here. Shea broke in with one final attempt: "Could I ask if you'd be willing to collaborate on the case, if it comes to that? It would be in our interest here to have a local firm handle some of the details, not having to soldier all the way up from Wexford at every turn."

Brady considered the offer for a long moment, took a puff on his pipe before answering, and replied: "I'm flattered, Phil, I really am. But I'm afraid I'll have to pass. You do understand why it might seem a bit disloyal for me to join Molly's team at this juncture?" Phil said he understood, and they left it at that.

Phil went straight to work on drafting a new letter to Carby, this one setting a deadline for a decision. He called the bull-necked courier, Mick Dolan, who was thrilled to deliver the news, relishing the rat-like terror in Carby's beady eyes as he spotted the yellow Land Rover, again, invading his driveway. He signed for the letter without a word, turned, and walked back inside the dingy kitchen, muttering under his breath: "Goddamn solicitors. Bloodsucking leeches."

This second solicitor's letter was crisp and to the point:

**March 23, 1988**

**Dear Mr. Bolger,**

**Over a month has elapsed since our letter of February 21, offering a generous, amicable settlement on the terms so described. We've had no response, though you've had ample time to consider the offer.**

The purpose of this letter is to inform you that you have until the 28th to decide. If we do not hear from you or your representative on or before the 28th, we will file for your eviction from the western half of Rathdangan farm—we will be surveying this within the week to establish an equitable division—before the circuit court in Kilkenny. The case will be presented before Judge Flanagan, with whose reputation you may be familiar. His judgment will then become binding and will be enforced by the Kilkenny garda.

That said, our preference is still to settle and move beyond the adversarial stance that your silence necessitates. This is our final offer and your last chance to respond in the affirmative. I urge you to seize this unique opportunity before it is too late.

Our deadline is 12 p.m., March 28, five days from today.

Sincerely yours,

E. Phillip O'Shea
Managing Partner

The deadline came and went with no response from Carby.

As promised, Phil Shea filed in the circuit court in Kilkenny for a writ to clear the western fields at Rathdangan farm for occupancy by the rightful owner. In the interest of community relations, Judge Flanagan decided to hold a hearing—unprecedented in such a case—for April 10, 1988. Good Friday, as it turned out.

The summons was delivered by the new garda, Micheal O'Toole, in a green envelope with the ominous seal of the court boldly displayed. Carby read the crisp letter slowly, then yelled "Fuckers!" at the top of his lungs before crunching the summons and tossing it in the fireplace. Raging, he smashed his right fist into the kitchen wall, fracturing two knuckles. His blood splattered across the kitchen table, staining the tablecloth and spoiling a newly baked loaf of soda bread. He wrapped the broken hand in a white towel, then drove the old McCormick tractor into town, parking it hastily in front of Finnegan's.

It was mid-afternoon on a dreary March Monday, the light coming back from its long hibernation. Carby shuffled in and sat up at the bar; he was my only customer in the pub, so I saw no harm in a bit of chat. The poor devil looked like he could use a friend, his beady eyes closer than usual, smoldering with confusion and resentment. He ordered a potent cocktail of painkillers and elixirs: a large Jameson and a pint of Guinness.

He gulped down the whiskey and ordered another, savoring the rush as the liquor hit his bloodstream. He fished for the Woodbines in his vest pocket, pulled one out, and lit up before launching: "The feckin' guards came out today wid a summons. Wants to drag me into court ta tell me ta get out, ta clear off me own farm? What da fuck have I done here ta be treated like a common criminal, defending what's mine? Tell me da truth, Myles Dunne... Do I look like a criminal ta you?"

"Not a bit, Carby," I assured him. "We all know you're a decent fella, from good stock, and there's no way you're a criminal. I'm sure Flanagan will be fair; that's why he didn't just order you off. Just be sure you have a good barrister in your corner, and all will be well."

He shook his head vehemently, and after a fit of coughing, replied:

"I don't... I don't have any feckin' barrister and I'm not gonna hav' wan. Der all da goddamn same... bunch o' bloodsuckers... take yer money an' drive off in der big feckin' Mercedes. No! I'll defend meself, an' if dat's not good enough, then so be it. Da truth is da truth. I don't need no suit ta spake for me."

I shrugged, wiped off a few glasses, and said, evenly: "That's up to you, Carby. I'm just sayin', if it was me, I'd want one o' those guys who can speak the lingo—if you follow me. The law can be very contrary; you never know what those boyos have up their sleeve."

"Yeah, well, I don't give one tinker's fart what dey have up their sleeve, or up their arse, for dat matter. Me

mind's made up; I'll have none o' dem bloodsuckers rob-
bin' me. Gimme another round here, Myles; dat Jameson
is a grand whiskey."

"Aye, 'tis, Carby, but I think you've had enough. If
yer gonna drive that tractor home, one-handed, I think
you'd better slow down. How about a glass o' Guinness?"

Carby's ebony eyes now burned with a glare of pure
hatred. He crushed the Woodbine under his boot and
leaned ominously across the counter. "Jaysus, Dunne!
Are you feckin' coddin' me? Yer cuttin' me off? Yer jes
like all da rest o' 'em! Well, ya can take yer drink and
shove it, for all I care. Yer all da same, ready ta kick a
fella when he's down. Wan a dese days, I'll show da lot a
yez! Dere's more ta dis t'ing dan meets da eye. Ye'll all be
sorry. Mark me words!"

With that, he flung a 10-pound note on the bar and
charged for the door. Pure Carby, his own worst enemy,
I reflected, as I turned to clear off his place and air the
pub out before the regulars arrived. The last I saw of
him was the black overcoat flying in the March wind, the
rusted tractor swerving down the main road toward the
stricken farm.

The hearing before Judge Flanagan took less than 30
minutes. Only about ten other people, huddled in pairs,
sat in the back two rows of the large, austere courtroom;
I drove the 18 miles to be there as a matter of curiosity, as

did a couple of close neighbors. Exiting the parking lot, I spotted Molly's long legs stepping out of Phil Shea's sleek BMW. She walked around the car and paused to brush some lint from his jacket and straighten his tie—followed by laughter and a reassuring pat on his chest. I felt a pang of jealousy at the intimacy of the gesture, Molly looking more like a lover than a client of the debonair barrister.

Inside the chilly courthouse, I immediately saw her again, seated at the long table in front, looking gorgeous in her tailored navy overcoat, with her blonde hair gleaming from under a yellow silk scarf. Phil, broad-shouldered and immaculately tailored, sat beside her, whispered to her once in a while, smiled, and patted her shoulder reassuringly. The nudges and chatter of the squinting window crowd, led by Peggy Carroll, was the only sound in the courtroom—their winks confirming the most sordid fantasies.

Carby lurked in the back, barely visible behind a few burly onlookers. He appeared pale and pathetic, head buried in his hands. He was alone, as usual.

Judge Flanagan strode in like a general on a reviewing parade. He was in his early seventies, with a full mane of silver hair and a commanding presence, his steely grey eyes scanning the room. The clerk jumped up and barked: "Everybody rise! Here comes the judge." We all scrambled to our feet, the clerk intoning: "Hear ye, hear ye. The circuit court of Kilkenny, presided over by the Honorable Judge Brian Flanagan, is now in session. You may be seated." We all dropped into our seats, with relief and a tingle of excitement at the drama about to unfold. From the back row of the sweltering courtroom, the only sound was a woman's hiccups.

The judge and Phil Shea seemed to know each other well, exchanging brief smiles of recognition and pleasantries before getting down to the cases on the docket. Bolger v. Bolger was first up.

Flanagan first heard Molly's ("the plaintiff's") case, delivered by her counsel—verbatim from his first letter to Carby. In a nutshell, Carby, Phil argued, was squatting on Noel's farm without permission and was doing so after making threats of violence against the executor, Molly, of Andy's will. But, in the interest of fairness and family harmony, she had generously handed Carby half the farm, in recognition of his years of labor. All he had to do was acknowledge the legitimacy of his father's will, sign a document acknowledging his debt for the other half, and agree to make the reasonable installment payments, as detailed in Phil's first letter.

I could hear a small rumble in the crowd, a grumbling sense of disapproval. Judge Flanagan jerked his wigged head up, clearly annoyed. He started to say something, but changed his mind. Instead, he simply expressed satisfaction with Phil's summation and smiled briefly toward the plaintiff's table, before pivoting, sharply, toward the defendant's table—where he expected to find Carby and his legal counsel.

But the table was empty: no Carby, no barrister, and no supporting cast. Flanagan glanced about, clearly livid; seeing no sign of Carby, he took an impatient, deep breath, and shouted: "Where is the defendant, Patrick Bolger? Is Mr. Bolger or his representative in the courtroom?" After what seemed an eternity, Carby identified himself from the back and muttered something about representing himself that we could barely make out. With a cold stare and a commanding flick of his right index finger, the judge ordered him to approach the bench.

Flanagan's first question was laced with annoyance: "Are you aware that you have a right to legal representation?" Carby, cap in hand, white collar and tie on top of a soiled shirt, shuffled forward, head bowed obsequiously.

Without making eye contact, he spoke in a stage whisper: "Yes, yer honor. I understand me rights on dat score."

Flanagan, with obvious agitation, pressed on: "Please speak up so that the court can hear you. Do you also understand that the results of today's hearing will be binding, that you cannot come back later and claim that you didn't get a fair hearing because you chose not to have such representation?"

"Yes, yer honor. I understand all dat."

"Fine, then let us proceed. What's your response to the charges Miss Bolger has brought and to her offer of amicability?"

Carby wrung the faded cap between his hands, as if he'd just washed it, and kept his eyes glued to the floor.

He spoke without raising his head: "Well, yer honor, as I've always said, and like me father before me, God rest his soul, I own dat farm—every blade o' grass, every fence post—as a matter o' custom. I'm da eldest son an' da farm is mine be law n' custom going back hundreds a years. Sure, no wan else has any rights or claims; dat's all up ta me. Me da told me so, many times."

Judge Flanagan shook his head in disbelief, made a few notes, took a sip of water, and turned a cold eye on Carby, as he might focus on an annoying bug he was about to squash. The hardened line on the judge's chiseled face suggested he was about to do just that.

"Do you have anything else to say in your defense?"

"Well, yer honor, sure me father was way too sick ta make a will; he was outa his mind wid pain from da cancer. If he was in his right mind, he'd 'ave known he couldn't just ignore ancient custom; ignore his only son. He'd never do dat, not Da. Dat's all dere is to it; sure everyone sez it's an open n' shut case. She has no rights, nor does the young lad. Women and der bastards have no rights in Ireland. It's just common sinse."

Flanagan, his face an inferno of disdain and annoyance, pushed a strand of his silver mane back under his wig before speaking. His voice now took on a darker tone, reserved for inferior beings who had the temerity to talk back to him.

"Well, it may be common sense to you, Mr. Bolger. And, astonishingly, it was common law for a long time, for over 600 years of Irish feudal history. But as times have changed, so has this law, which was, of course, profoundly discriminatory toward women in particular, and to younger siblings who were often deserving of recompense for a life of toil—all uncompensated."

Judge Flanagan looked at Carby, took another sip of water, and met Phil Shea's eyes with a knowing, insider's look, before continuing.

"In this case, though she might have brought you to court and won, your sister has been more than generous under the circumstances. And your father had the wisdom to leave a clear will, which is perfectly legal and dispositive. The beneficiary of his will was absolutely Andrew Bolger's choice, and there is no evidence whatsoever that your father was impaired or coerced. Quite the contrary. We have a fully witnessed and notarized affidavit to certify to his soundness of mind, and therefore, the legality of his will in favor of his grandson."

At this point, Carby could contain himself no longer. He jumped up, flung his cap on the floor, and cut off Flanagan's peroration abruptly:

"No feckin' way in hell!" He shouted this so that even those in the balcony could hear him clearly. "The man had ta be outa his mind. Everywan knows dat. Everywan! Except you and dis crowd here," pointing an accusing finger in Molly and Phil's direction.

To our general amazement, Judge Flanagan let Carby finish without admonition. Instead, he took a deep breath, raised his eyes toward the ceiling, as if pleading for patience, then continued as though he hadn't heard a word of Carby's outburst.

"I've carefully considered the merits of the case, and I find your sister's offer to be extraordinarily generous under the circumstances. Why you can't appreciate that fact escapes me, but that's for you to ponder. Meanwhile, this court orders you to vacate the western 20 acres as set out from the survey at Rathdangan farm, to desist from further threats to your sister or her son, and, if you should decide to accept the offer being made, pay half the value of the farm including all its assets as an estate, which, as executor, she will determine at her sole discretion." Flanagan paused, looked to see how Carby was taking it, and pressed on.

"All payments must be made in full by October 1 of this year, 1988. In the meantime, it is Miss Bolger's decision whether and under what conditions she allows you future access to these fields at Rathdangan farm. As noted, she has already offered to include the farmhouse, outbuildings, implements, and livestock as part of the bargain. It's now up to you to recognize a good thing when you see it. Your sister's decision will be binding on you within 24 hours of this notice and will be enforced by the garda at her request. This court stands adjourned!"

With that, Judge Flanagan banged his gavel, gathered his papers, and strode briskly toward his chambers.

Molly rose, smiled at Phil, planted a soft kiss on his cheek, and whispered something in his ear. He smiled, nodded, and packed his papers into the well-worn leather briefcase, then ushered her out of the courtroom, like a man in charge. And in love.

The squinting window crowd, now free to slander at will, huddled in the balcony like a pack of evil alchemists, spinning scurrilous innuendo into gospel truth. Their leader, Peggy Carroll—always on the alert for juicy bits—spoke with all the delicacy of a fishmonger: "Did ya see that brazen hussy? Kissing yer man right in front o' da judge? Sure dat woman has no shame. No shame. Maybe wan a dese days Mister Shea will make an honest woman of 'er, now dat de cat is outa de bag." The gaggle of old crones joined the chorus set up by Peggy, adding juicy tidbits of gossip she might have missed or understated.

I felt nauseated hearing this claptrap broadcast across the courtroom. It was all I could do not to toss the lot of them headfirst off the balcony. Instead, I ducked out for the Leinster Arms across the street, to drown my sorrows, and hope against hope that I was reading too much into what I'd just witnessed.

On the way out, I glanced over at Carby, sunk lower at the table, head buried in his crossed forearms. For a moment, I thought I saw his shoulders heave in a sob. I couldn't help but feel sorry for the poor wretch, but dared not approach him in public, not knowing how he might react. One thing I did know: This was really going to get messy now. Flanagan's ruling had set the table for unmitigated mischief, as if willfully, maliciously unleashing the hounds of hell from the darker recesses of Carby's tormented soul.

At this time of year—the spring season—the banter at Finnegan's would normally be dominated by planting, sheep, and hurling: Who was sowing what in which field? What outrageous price had seed corn and fertilizer soared to? What price might fat lambs bring? And, liveliest of all, who was going to make it all the way to the All-Ireland Hurling Final at Croke Park in September?

This year, that was all brushed aside. Instead, the pub became a kind of makeshift courtroom, with me, Myles Dunne, host to nightly rounds of impassioned arguments on the gross injustice done to Carby Bolger—and, by proxy, to the rest of Rathdangan—by Flanagan's ruling. "The Court at Finnegan's" (our informal handle) was much more thorough than was Flanagan's Court at Kilkenny. After two months, we were still calling witnesses, though the self-selected barristers and jury of regulars had long since made up their minds.

The overwhelming majority thought Carby got a raw deal. After all, just about every farmer in Ireland had inherited his land under the aegis of primogeniture. Carby was right: It was just taken for granted; "common sinse," as he'd put it to Judge Flanagan. The most common rhetorical question was: "Why should some tart and her bastard son destroy such a fine, fair-minded tradition?" And one thing seemed obvious: Andy Bolger must have been out o' his mind. No sane man would make such a will, destroying his own son, not to mention the community he loved, with one stroke of a pen.

"Well, for the umpteenth time, I'll tell yez gobshites why…" came the booming voice of Darby Breen, self-appointed sage who'd spent one year at University College, Galway (UCG) before dropping out to follow his first love: poetry. Since then, he'd been vociferous prosecutor of all things traditional. He was on his third pint and second month of being the sole voice in favor of Judge Flanagan's ruling.

Taking a deep draught, Darby launched into his familiar speech. We all knew it by heart at this point: "Times have changed; see, here in the Republic of Ireland we're no longer under Brehon Law or British rule, where primogeniture was a fixture for centuries. Sure it was set up to keep royalty and dictators in power *in perpetuity*—that's Latin, meaning forever; now that's a quare long time, if ya ask me. Now, as a free people, we follow our own constitution, the one Padraig Pearse drew up in 1916, which guaranteed equality to all the people of Ireland. It never said to favor the eldest son; that's the rub here, see. And that's why…"

Seamus Barry, an unmarried laborer with no land, was sick of Darby's pontificating. Barry knew injustice when he saw it, and this, for him, was a clear-cut case: "Whoa! Hould yer horses dere, Darby! Show me where it's written in da Irish constitution dat a man should give up his land to a woman an' her bastard son just cuz she's done what she's supposed ta do n' care for her elderly Mammy an' Daddy?"

Darby, a man with a keen sense of his own infallibility, was not going to suffer this fool gladly. He rolled his eyes, as though speaking to a slow child, and raised his voice as though the slow child was also hard of hearing: "Listen to me! Sure yer talking like the feckin' eejit that y'are, Barry. The law is never specific like that; it lays out principles, guidelines, that have to be tailored to each situation. And the principle of equality is well established in the Irish Republic by now; that's why Flanagan needed no time to decide."

Barry looked around for support, hoping someone would jump in on his side. He knew he was out of his depth, but he couldn't just let Darby call him an "eejit" and say nothing. He suddenly thought of a new tack: "How do you know how long it took him to decide? Maybe he made the wrong decision. Did ya ever consider that?"

Darby brushed him off, like a gnat, with a dismissive wave of his free hand.

"Listen, gobshite, there was no decision to be made. Flanagan had already made up his mind. Ya wouldn't know this, but Phil Shea's da and Judge Flanagan were roommates and all-star ruggers at Trinity College—they were known as Mr. Inside and Mr. Outside—after their running styles. Been fast friends ever since; families still vacation together in France every summer. There's no way Flanagan is going to rule against anywan Phil Shea or his firm represents. Carby was banjaxed before he ever set foot in that courtroom. He was smart not to waste money on a barrister."

Paddy Crotty, our TD (representative in parliament), a born orator and respected farmer with 90 acres up near Brandon, had heard enough from Darby, a man he despised as a layabout on the dole:

"If ya listen to Breen's blather, ya'd t'ink we were still a feckin' British colony, still singing God Save the Queen. We just have to lie down and take whatever the powers dat be sez. And, according to Mister Breen, the rest of us here are no bether than landgrabbers an' carpet-baggers." The crowd fell silent as Crotty took the floor, warming to his topic. "No mather dat our forefathers fought an' died for every square inch of dis little island; no mather dat de Fenians an' Republican Brotherhood had ta take ta de hills an' fight wid pikes against cannons ta liberate us from de murderous Redcoats; no mather dat our forefathers an' fathers before us worked dere fingers ta de bone so we could hav' somethin' we could call our own—land ta take a stand on."

Crotty had won four consecutive elections with this brand of rabble-rousing nationalism. The crowd was feeling the contagion of the mob—standing shoulder-to-shoulder in solidarity, hoping to catch the All-Ireland broadcast between Kilkenny and Wexford. Crotty's voice dropped to an ominous growl as he moved in for the kill on Darby, his cornered adversary.

"You an' yer ilk—the infernal Flanagans of this world—is tellin' us ta obey da law an' move wid da times. And I say we've heard dis before, for over 700 years, from John Bull's henchmen an' informers. An' me answer is da same as ever: TA HELL WITH DA LAW n' da times if dat's what it's telling me. As Carby sez, 'Over me fucken dead body.' No way! Never! NEVER!" This at the top of his lungs. Then he closed, in a sinister growl: "They can all go ta hell. Up the Republic!"

Crotty had hit paydirt, as he knew he would. The crowd roared its approval:

"Hear! Hear! The man spakes da truth. Let's drink ta Carby and to Crotty's Declaration." Long and raucous applause echoed through the empty street in sleepy Rathdangan. I knew this was great for business, and I wanted to encourage it, so I bought another round "on the house," as anxiety morphed into outrage at the obvious injustice Judge Flanagan, a clear outsider, had perpetrated against one of our own, our upstanding friend Carby Bolger.

In the weeks following this near insurrection, Carby became the center of attention, with a loyal, vociferous following. He seemed like a new man, even smiling once in a while, trying on this unfamiliar role, a genuine *cause célèbre*. Carby, if not quite a hero, was now a man to be reckoned with, and—fair play to him—he seized the day with both hands.

Each night found him sauntering into Finnegan's early, where people jostled each other for a ringside seat, as the new Carby held forth at the bar, no longer hiding out in his isolated cubby. He still ordered two pints at once, now free—compliments of well-wishers and a small army of self-appointed experts on legal defense strategy.

Behind the bar, I resolutely stayed above the fray, saying little, busier than ever. The consensus strategy for Carby was defiance, pure and simple. Stonewall Flanagan's eviction order, the crowd advised, and let the devil take the hindmost. This stance came natural to a people with a strong, recent memory of the colonial yoke. It fired every fevered hindbrain, and silenced the only vocal dissenter, Darby Breen.

Over the weeks, the regulars had taken on an ominous tone, shifting from spirited debating club to inflamed, vengeful, mob—chanting as one. No longer tolerant of devil's advocates, the usual suspects came to the fore. Their voices grew hoarse each night repeating the same bad advice, the same litany of reasons Carby was on firm footing, and the rock-solid conviction that Judge Flanagan was corrupt and evil. What was Flanagan going to do: send in the garda to boot him out? They knew Molly would never allow that to happen to her own flesh and blood. And, as the mob repeated, over and over: "Ya can't squeeze blood from a turnip." Carby had no money, and Flanagan wouldn't evict him without at least another hearing.

This time, Carby wouldn't be alone; he'd be armed with a team of distinguished barristers—pro bono volunteers, according to the hoarse, Guinness-fueled voices at Finnegan's—with the entire Rathdangan community in his corner. With each iteration of the case and each free round of drinks at the bar, I could see Carby morph, as if by magic, from hapless victim to proud landowner; from foul-smelling freak to local hero; from desperate defendant to defiant crusader.

I was feeling increasingly on edge about the tone at Finnegan's. Molly was on my mind, as usual, and I was worried how all this was going to turn out for her, for Carby, and for the boy, Noel. Many a night, especially near closing time, after they'd had one too many, and Paddy Crotty had whipped the pub into a frenzy, I was tempted to call the garda to calm things down.

At last the court deadline came into view. October first was just a week away, and Carby had made it clear to one-and-all that he had no intention of complying with Judge Flanagan's ruling. "Feck Flanagan; he had no right to order me off me own land; he can kiss me arse. I'll die defending every bit o' land before I cough up a penny o' dere blood money. Sure they'll only get me outa dere in a box." This was the essence of the speech he delivered every night—sometimes several times, with various riffs and embellishments on the "blood money" theme—to his widening circle of fans at the pub.

Finnegan's was a different place now, with standing-room-only crowds every night of the week. The word had spread and people came from far and near to take in Carby's act. Watching him from behind the bar, I marveled at this charming, verbose incarnation, one no one who knew him as I did would have recognized a few short weeks earlier. This was a miraculous case of human transformation: The new Carby was a man of confidence; a man of pride; a man of stature; a man of wit; and above all, a man of conviction and courage. How could this be happening, right here at Finnegan's?

He seemed taller, too—by several inches, it seemed—cap pushed back at a jaunty angle, like Johnny Hooker, Robert Redford's character in *The Sting.* Gone was the distinctive, sulfuric body odor; and his eyes—once dark, darting, and beady—seemed livelier, steadier, and much larger. They'd even seemed to have changed color, to a green-tinged light brown.

We talked about little else but Carby, expressing our collective amazement, shaking our heads incredulously. We knew we were witnessing some kind of once-in-a-lifetime metamorphosis, but no one believed it was real. It was as though we were living a fantasy, a dream from which we'd all awake only to find the real Carby back in his stall by the back door, smelling putrid as ever. Given how we'd treated him over the years, we all felt a bit ashamed, too. Had we not all secretly cheered for Andy's will—disgusted as we were by *that* Carby—the first time we'd heard about it?

The October 1ˢᵗ deadline, like the others, came and went without incident. No change in Carby's position: He was standing firm. No word from Molly, Phil Shea, or Judge Flanagan. Two weeks went by, and the latest rumor at Finnegan's was that Molly had changed her mind and was engaged to Phil Shea—a rumor that cost me countless sleepless nights as I cursed my own cowardice and lack of self-confidence.

When the rumor turned out to be bogus, I made a vow that I was going to find some way to get that blonde beauty's attention. But how? As I've said, she never came in the pub or went to the dances. And I certainly didn't have the nerve to knock on her door and ask her for a date.

By All Saints' Day, October 31ˢᵗ, the word at Finnegan's was that Carby was in the clear. People were buying rounds in celebration, clapping him on the back as though he'd just scored the winning goal in the All-Ireland Final. Now a relaxed, crowd-pleasing raconteur, with his own brand of wit and a vast storehouse of ghost stories, fables, and anecdotes, Carby was hands-down the marquee attraction at the pub. He ran up a steep tab, which worried me, but Uncle Tommy thought it worth the risk, given how much business Carby attracted—all for free.

That was before the garda served Carby with a second summons from Judge Flanagan.

The summons came in the usual funereal, court-sealed envelope. Michael O'Toole, the fresh-faced garda, was a bit taken aback at Carby's new appearance, hardly recognizing him as the same cowed figure he'd seen back in April. Carby took the summons calmly, signed for it, and slapped O'Toole heartily on the back. "Don't worry about it, Sir. I know ya must hate delivering dese auld yokes ta people. Sure someone has ta do it. No hard feelins; yer only doin' yer job."

The summons took half a page of dreary green parchment:

**November 4, 1988**

**Patrick E. Bolger of Rathdangan town land is hereby held in contempt of court and is ordered to appear in the circuit court of the county of Kilkenny before presiding judge, the Honorable Brian Flanagan, on the 15ᵗʰ Day of November, 1988, to face sentencing. This court seeks full compliance with the court order of April 10ᵗʰ inst., either in the form of a cashier's cheque for the sum of £50,000 or a notarized affidavit accepting the decision of this court, to wit: Molly Bolger is the executor of the family farm holdings at Rathdangan and has, by order of this court, decreed that you must vacate the premises**

**immediately following the court hearing. In the absence of a cashier's cheque, the entire farm— including farmhouse, implements, livestock, etc.—will be put to public auction and sold to the highest bidder at the earliest feasible date following the hearing. The distribution of the proceeds will be at the absolute discretion of the executor, after administrative expenses are paid.**

Carby showed up at Finnegan's that night in high spirits. He passed the summons around proudly, doing a hilarious standup routine mimicking the pompous Judge Flanagan, with a pseudo-British accent:

"Now, my good fellow. Are you aware that I will kick your culchie arse all the way to Rosslare Harbor if you dare to stand up for your rights?"

At this point, Carby would wring his cap pitifully, head bowed, mimicking his former self, before answering:

"Yis, yer honor. Sure I almost shit meself whin I got yer fierce edict. I sez ta meself, sez I, tis a pity Judge Flanagan don't know who da feck he's daling wid here. So, try dis? Go fuck yourself n' de horse ya rode in an, if ye'll excuse me French. It's just our way o' spakin' down here. Culchie talk. Don't expect ya ta follow. Would ya care fer wan a dem auld translators?"

Gales of laughter convulsed the regulars up and down the bar, followed by a hearty ovation: "Hear! Hear! No bether man! Pull dat man another pint dere, Myles. It's an me."

Carby was clearly the man of the hour. Next he'd be running for TD, taking Paddy Crotty's job.

In the midst of it all, with winter coming on, we braced for the dreaded gloom in the change of seasons. The golden fields of autumn were now a poignant memory, replaced by a stubbly, gray landscape, and the toneless chant of the whippoorwill in the rushes. Winter announced herself abruptly, like a nasty schoolmistress in a bad mood, eager to show her disdain for this soggy North Atlantic outlier. She barely allowed us daylight, which came grudgingly late, if at all, and was off the job before mid-afternoon each day. On either side of these meager sightings, she shrouded us in a thick blanket of fog, rising lazily off the Barrow, before unfurling her curtain of inky blackness on the village, leaving us to endure another endless night in the shadow of the Blackstairs Range.

The mood at Finnegan's darkened, too, as the November 15th hearing approached. Advice flowed from every quarter, most of it incoherent and contradictory. The *pro bono* barristers—so abundant in summer, though never named—were now missing in action, as were all those willing to "die for Ireland," "post bail," or "kick in whatever it takes" for Carby's defense.

Still, though more muted, the crowd converged on a consistent position: defiance. It was summed up by the agitator-in-chief, Paddy Crotty: "Feck 'em! Don't even bother to show. What are they gonna do? Throw ya off yer own farm?"

Darby Breen, the loyal opposition, reminded him that a no-show could result in his arrest and eviction. "Fair point," Carby conceded, "But where the feck am I gonna get 50,000 pounds? Sure they can't squeeze blood from a turnip." This was the gist of Carby's logic, night after night, as all heads bobbed in violent agreement.

Besides, they couldn't sell the farm "out from under him" without a transfer of title, and that hadn't happened; not yet. That was the last ray of hope: The farm was still in Andy Bolger's name, as far as anyone could tell. Anyway—and, after all the talk, they always came full-circle to this comforting thought: "Possession is 90% of the law; as long as ya show up to court, they can't evict ya." Worst case scenario, Carby, they all agreed, would still get half the farm. Even Molly had already agreed that this was "only fair." This whole thing could take years to work out. Time was on Carby's side in this. And Judge Flanagan wasn't getting any younger...

Assured by this "reasoning" and confident of his position, Carby abandoned any vague notion of getting legal advice. If push came to shove, he would face Flanagan alone, again.

Meanwhile, Carby went about his workaday life as if nothing had changed. He seemed busier than ever, digging trenches down by the Barrow—we had no idea what they were for—tending the livestock, and being a good steward of the land. With cash from a good wheat harvest, grown on the western meadows, he bought a new suit for the showdown. There was a 50% sale on men's Italian suits at McNally's in Kilkenny. He also bought a blue shirt and bright floral tie, at the suggestion of the buxom sales clerk—a perky girl named Breda, who smelled exotic, smiled a lot, gently righted his turned-up collar, and called him Mr. Bolger. For the first time in his life, Carby felt attractive to a woman. With a spring in his step, he felt ready to face Judge Flanagan.

Maybe he'd come back and get Breda's phone number after the hearing. Maybe he'd tell her his real name was Patrick, not Carby. Bring her a bunch o' lilacs. Start fresh, a new man.

He talked about his crush at length at Finnegan's, and we imagined Carby, an Irish Casanova, sweeping a bevy of Kilkenny girls off their feet and, years from now, writing his "Memoirs"—as had the original Italian playboy—for all the world to nudge and wink over at the "naughty bits." Watching him step into the pub every night with his newfound swagger, this image was not out of the question.

This time, Carby's hearing was packed and noisy. His popularity and the wrath engendered by Flanagan's ruling brought an audience of all stripes, eager to see the fur fly. The press occupied a whole row, some with vaunted credentials: *The Irish Times, The Irish Press, Radio Television Eireann (RTE),* and all the local and regional media. There was standing-room-only 30 minutes before

the court was called to order, the din sounding more like
a cattle mart than a courtroom.

The clerk had to call us to order three times before
we paid any attention. It took Flanagan's fierce glare to
finally bring full silence as we all stood for his entrance.
This time, only three people sat at the front tables. Molly
had decided not to come; Phil and a young solicitor from
the firm were there to represent her. Carby, sporting his
new, teal-green Italian suit and bright floral tie, still sat
alone. He looked over at Phil and smiled politely. I noticed Phil whisper something to his colleague, who then
strained to get a better look at Carby. Like the rest of us,
Phil may not have believed what he saw: a well-dressed,
confident-looking man, smiling congenially, as though
greeting close friends.

There was only one other case before Bolger v. Bolger
this time. We listened half-heartedly as Flanagan handed
out stiff fines to an errant motorist, suspending his driver's license for a year for 25 unpaid parking tickets. He
owed something around 300 quid.

"And now, Mr. Kilpatrick," Flanagan intoned, "you
may walk to the bank for a cashier's cheque made out
to the Department of Traffic Regulation, Goresbridge,
Co. Kilkenny. It's due no later than November 30th.
Your driver's license is suspended for two years—
until December 1st, 1990. And don't let me see you back
here again, for any reason. Blackguards like you give me
hives."

Finally, it was Carby's turn. All eyes turned to Flanagan as he read his notes, adjusted his wig, and focused his stern gaze on the new Carby, who made easy eye contact and smiled.

"Mr. Bolger," Flanagan began curtly. "I understand that you have chosen to defy the order of this court in meeting the requirements we established at the last hearing. Do you have anything to say by way of explanation? Perhaps extenuating circumstances?"

Carby set his cap on the table and stood, shoulders squared, almost handsome in his new attire. He looked straight at the judge, cleared his throat, and launched: "Well, yer honor, I've thought a lot about yer decision, and I wasn't tryin' to defy it; I just didn't know what ta do about it, since I don't have that kinda money ta buy half da farm. I agree that me sister has worked hard, was good ta Mammy and Daddy, rest their souls, an' dat she an' da young lad now own da farm. But I don't t'ink she ever wanted ta break up da farm, as I understand her t'inkin'."

Carby paused to let this sink in, looking at the judge for a reaction. Seeing none, he decided to press on with his proposal: "So if I could give her half da earnings a da farm every year till it gets ta what she t'inks is fair, dat way I could afford it n' da farm would stay in da family. Maybe by den, da young lad would want ta farm it an' keep it going…"

With that, Carby stopped, smiled hopefully—looking boyish, and held judge Flanagan's unblinking stare for several seconds.

"Do you have anything else you wish to add, Mr. Bolger?"

"No, yer honor. Dat's it. I hope ye'll see me p'int o' view."

A murmur of approval rose up around the courtroom; someone in the gallery shouted: "Good man, Carby. Dat's da stuff!" Carby blushed, lifting his palms up and down in a pleading gesture of cooling it. This was a delicate moment; he did not need any red flags waved in front of Judge Flanagan's baleful glare.

But it was too late.

Incensed, Flanagan turned his fury on the gallery:

"Garda, clear the gallery of these hooligans immediately! I'll have no rabble-rousers in my courtroom. Any further demonstration and I'll clear the court. I hope that's understood."

Without waiting for the result, he looked at Phil Shea, whom he beckoned to approach the bench. They conferred *sotto voce* for a moment, Phil listening and nodding in agreement with whatever the judge was proposing. Then Phil sat and whispered to his junior colleague, who promptly left the courtroom before Judge Flanagan addressed Carby once more.

"Mr. Bolger, I've duly noted your change of tone and demeanor since your last appearance in this court. It is to be admired; emotional maturation is always to be encouraged, however late its emergence. Unfortunately, it's a case of too little, too late. Your offer is of no interest to the plaintiff, being impossible to measure, with no guarantee of ever being implemented." Flanagan paused and glanced at Carby, who stood impassively, taking in every word without reaction.

Flanagan forged ahead with his peroration: "What you are asking is for your sister and her son to shoulder the risks of the farm, gamble on its future success, without any recognition of her past services and *de facto* full ownership. Given the family history and the vagaries of farming, especially this particular farm, the plaintiff finds it an unacceptable risk and deems it *absolutely* out of the question."

To drive the point home, Flanagan slammed his palm on the bench, glaring at Carby and the crowded courtroom, inviting defiance. Seeing none from either source, he continued. "In light of the fact that you have not met the requisite condition of a cash settlement, I hereby honor Mr. O'Shea's request, and order that you vacate the premises immediately, by noon tomorrow, and that those lands be put to public auction not later than April 15, 1989, and that said land be sold to the highest bidder with no reserve bids."

Flanagan glared at Carby as he issued his ultimatum, expecting an outcry or some sign of defiance. All he saw was a calm-faced farmer listening intently, nodding his understanding.

Surprised, Flanagan paused—seeming flustered—fumbling through his notes before closing.

"Again, at the plaintiff's request, I have assigned the auction to J. M. Tobin & Sons, Valuers and Auctioneers,

Enniscorthy, Co. Wexford, who will represent the interest of the owner until the sale is completed. You are hereby ordered to vacate the designated premises immediately and are cautioned not to interfere with the logistics of the sale under pain of arrest. The garda is hereby enjoined to enforce this eviction notice. Don't let me see you back here! This court stands adjourned!"

With that, Flanagan stood, looked straight at the hostile crowd—who'd started a loud grumbling in the gallery—and stared them into submission. His military bearing and vociferous body language sent an unmistakable message: "Don't even think about it!" If anyone did, they didn't show it; most avoided his belligerent stare, looking at the ground or scanning the nearest exit.

Once satisfied that the crowd was brought to heel, Flanagan packed his briefcase and strode deliberately back to his chambers. The courtroom emptied quickly. No one spoke a word. They'd hold their vitriol for another venue: post time at Finnegan's.

By nightfall, after the first couple of rounds, the indignation knew no bounds. If I hadn't been in the courtroom, I might have believed that it had been a scene of brazen defiance, Flanagan narrowly escaping a lynching.

Paddy Crotty had his stock historical references: "Sure I was about ta tell that prick to go feck himself. Dis is still a free country; we're not under Stalin or Mao, ya know. And Hitler lost da war, as far as I can tell. Am I not right?"

Sean Finnegan, whose courage knew no bounds after two pints, agreed: "Exactly so, Paddy. That auld fucker in his wig n' robes has no right takin' da bread from a hard-working man's mouth. Sell the land right out from under us, is what he's doin'.... Dat's not right. Dere must be a law agin' dat. If I didn't t'ink it would've led ta bloodshed, I'd have jumped in an' tauld Mr. Brian Flanagan where to get off. He must t'ink we're all a bunch of feckin' eejits, staring at us like dat. I stared right back—did ya see dat?—till he backed down n' left da room. I'm not afeared o' anywan."

His drinking buddy, Matt Murphy, was more philosophical: "Begob, Flanagan's quare lucky we're all law abidin' citizens, or he'd 'ave been torn from limb ta limb in dere. It was touch an' go for a while, I'll tell ya; Sean had ta hauld me back, an' I know he was ready ta go as well. He tauld me dat over at J.P. Floods afterwards, n' dat's da God's honest truth."

Others jumped in, all speaking at once, with fervent testimonials of their super-human restraint in the face of such provocation. In the end, it all came down to one conclusion: Judge Flanagan was one lucky S.O.B. to have escaped with his life.

That night, Carby was quiet, but didn't withdraw to his cubby. He sat at the end of the bar, sipped his Guinness, and took it all in stride, still in his new Italian suit, tie loosened, not looking at all like a man who'd just been evicted from his farm. Instead, Carby smiled acknowledgments and shook hands as people offered their commiseration and advice.

Nothing raised a man's standing in Rathdangan faster than arbitrary justice at the hands of the powers that be. We loved our martyrs—so solidarity was now the order of the day. Every tactic of sabotage, short of assassination—from an armed militia to scaring off surveyors and auctioneers, to boycotting the auction—was given an elaborate public airing.

Arguments raged back and forth over each gambit, but one clear notion they all agreed on: one of their own—and therefore the whole village—had suffered a terrible injustice, and they would not back down an inch. No! Never! This would be a fight to the death, if necessary. Beyond that sentiment, details were in short supply, as were personal commitments, like the army of *pro bono* legal heavy weights who'd never materialized at Carby's hearing.

Over the next few months, as the days grew longer, and spring approached in all her verdant splendor, we breathed a collective sigh of relief after the dark, interminable winter. Carby's predicament was trumped by more immediate concerns. Planting season was upon Rathdangan, which this year had more than its usual challenges: The price of all the cash crops—milk, wheat, sugar beet, cattle, lambs, poultry—was being undercut by a glut of European and Australian imports.

Darby Breen offered his trenchant opinion: "Sure it doesn't even make sense to plant a crop anymore when we can't even count on covering our costs. What's a man supposed to live on, scenery?" This from a landless poet who did exactly that.

For all the talk, we knew everyone was going to plant. The question was, when? The greatest worry card was how to get the plowing done in the face of ruinous floods in the river valley, exacerbated by a rare snowstorm in late January that blocked the roads for weeks. Over 500 people died across the island, most on the west coast. Unprepared for such emergencies in remote regions of the island, old people in poor health and sickly infants, often living in isolation, had not held out for long—in spite of valiant attempts at rescue.

Rathdangan was lucky in not losing a single soul, but most of the local farmers, including Carby, lost over half their livestock—mostly ewes with young lambs—in the massive drifts that mimicked the hulking profile of the Blackstairs Mountains in the background. Faced with such widespread hardship, tales of the Great Hunger of the 1840s were recounted, as daily heroics and neighborly generosity reminded us all how lucky we were to live in this community.

Meanwhile, Molly Bolger and her son, Noel, seemed to have disappeared into thin air. It was all the buzz at Finnegan's that she'd eloped to America with Phil Shea—the rumored sire of Noel—leaving Carby with yet another reprieve. No one had seen her for weeks around Goresbridge. Her apartment over Cavanagh's Hardware seemed abandoned, letters spilling out of the mailbox.

This was the squinting window's favorite fantasy, with all the makings of an epic myth: illicit sex, disputed inheritance, family feud, courtroom drama, injustice, mystery, romance, anguish, and sacrifice, now to be redeemed by a romantic, happy ending. For the second time since November, I fought off despair as the rumor took hold, conjuring ways to keep up appearances at the thought of never seeing those blue eyes again. Or, seeing them in a new woman, Mrs. Phillip O'Shea.

My descent into melancholy was sharply arrested by incredible news from my American literary agent: He'd secured an American publisher and a generous advance for my first novel. When he called with the news, I thought I was hallucinating, after over a decade of obscurity as a writer and a drawer full of rejection slips.

This time, Skip Carroll—my upbeat and energetic agent who'd always believed in my writing talent, even when I'd had my doubts—came up trumps. With the advance, I could quit my job at Finnegan's and write full-time, a dream I'd harbored for years of scraping and scrounging. I wouldn't leave Uncle Tommy in the lurch, but I promised myself to give notice as soon as Carby's case was settled.

Skip flew in from New York, and we celebrated all night on a Dublin pub crawl that began at Davy Byrne's on

Duke Street—famous for its mention in Joyce's *Ulysses*—and ended at a dingy after-hours club on Leeson Street. The hangover lasted me for days, as did the smell of Havana cigars and the taste of McCallan's Scotch. Still, well worth it.

After I broke the news at Finnegan's, Darby Breen shrugged dismissively and muttered, "That's grand. Sure, now ye'll be a famous author, Myles, a regular Bernie Shaw (aka, George Bernard); ye won't want to talk to the likes of us…" Then the regulars went right back to heroic declarations on what they would have done if push came to shove with Molly's ultimatum and what this meant for the Carby/Flanagan standoff. Perhaps now she'd call off the dogs and give her fine, upstanding brother a break?

As usual, Paddy Crotty captured the prevailing sentiment: "Sure, everyone knows Phil Shea is rollin' in dough; some say he may even be a millionaire! Molly and the young lad will never want for anythin' from here on out, as the wife and adopted son of a rich man. An' sure, Phil won't expect a dowry. That girl's face is her fortune, like her mother before her—a ravin' beauty. He'll make a dacent woman of her and give that young lad a respectable name. Bejaysus, it's a great match."

"Hear! Hear! Let's drink ta Phil n' Molly." The whole pub joined in the chorus. Once again, Carby was back in the center of things, upgraded to "fine and upstanding," being feted with free rounds on news of this fortuitous turn of events. I just stood there with a frozen smile, incredulous, going through the motions, fighting off spasms of nausea and a limbic sense of despair.

As it turned out, both were unwarranted, as was the celebration. Phil Shea was photographed by the *Evening Herald* at a golf tournament in Enniscorthy; apparently, he'd never been away in the first place. It was Molly who was away—in the U.S. She'd taken Noel to visit his aunts, deciding to stay, "as long as she bloody well feels like it," as one of the regulars declared impatiently, after being asked "How long is she gone for?" once too often.

No one really knew, but it made for great craic to have so many making as if they had the inside track. It never dawned on any of us to ask: "How do you know that?" Much more fun to argue about things we knew nothing about. One thing was clear: Carby was still in Flanagan's crosshairs, still under an eviction notice, still defiant. He showed no sign of going anywhere and continued to enjoy his outlaw status in Rathdangan.

That was about to change, though none of us could have imagined the chain of events that were about to unfold.

Like the unmistakable sound of the first cuckoo in late spring—signaling bad news for her unsuspecting prey—the harbinger in the Bolger's case arrived on May Day, this time in the form of an American tourist.

I knew this guy from my days tending bar in New York City. Not personally, but the type—the way he strode in, like the leader of a gang of the Hell's Angels invading a small town diner, exuding trouble. He wore a green T-shirt, with *Pog Mo Thoin* (Kiss My Arse) emblazoned across the front; leprechauns and dwarfs with top hats and rude gestures adorned the back. Beefy, in his late fifties, he was about 5´10˝, with massive forearms, no neck, and a sandy crew cut. His pale blue eyes scanned the pub suspiciously, and it struck me that he could be a cop, a bouncer, or a bounty hunter. An ugly red scar disfigured the left side of his face, advertising a violent brush with fate.

He was followed by a woman in her late thirties, a tall brunette with too much makeup, straight, silky hair down her back, and sullen brown eyes. Behind the couple came two strapping young men, both around 6´4˝, in their mid-twenties, clearly identical twins, with freckles and flaming red hair down to their shoulders. Unlike their da, they were strikingly handsome, with perfect teeth, laughing and punching each other boisterously over some private joke. Except for the da, the family looked liked an ad in an Irish travel brochure. All wore touristy T-shirts—each one more offensive than the next—the kind the Irish wouldn't be caught dead wearing: "Erin Go Braless!"

I took their orders quietly, wary of the bellicose body language. The men ordered Guinness, of course; the woman, "A Bombay G 'n T, with a twist." She looked out the window and yawned audibly as she gave her order; bored and rude, I thought, as I smiled at her. I struck up the requisite small talk with the men, about the weather, the recent snow storm, and the prospects for fishing in the river Barrow.

It turned out that they were no mere tourists; they were in Rathdangan on a mission, one the da soon revealed in a clipping from the *Irish Times*. It read: "For Sale by Public Auction: 20-acre farm at Rathdangan, Co. Kilkenny. Farmhouse, outbuildings, livestock and implements. River and road access. Sale to highest bidder. No reserve. Auction at the Kildara Arms, Kilkenny City Center, May 25, 1989, 2 p.m. Enquiries for showing: J.M. Tobin, Valuers and Auctioneers, Enniscorthy, Co. Wexford." As usual, the April deadline was taken as more of a guideline than a court order. We never hurried things in Rathdangan, even for ferocious Judge Flanagan.

His name was Kevin Cassidy. His wife was Sarah, and the twins, "my boys," were Seamus and Sean. I wondered what happened to their mother. Cassidy's Irish ancestors were from Galway, on the west coast; this was his first visit to "the auld country." He still felt a "sentimental attachment" to Ireland and was interested in buying some land, an investment for his sons as well as for the sentimental value of saying they owned a bit of the "Auld Sod." This delivered with theatrical body language and a pitiful attempt at an Irish brogue.

They'd been to the U.K. already and seemed very proud of a brand new Jaguar they'd bought "off the showroom floor" in London and were shipping back to the U.S. Driving into the village, they'd been delayed by a convoy of traveling people camping by the roadside, and this had aroused Cassidy's ire: "What's with these goddamned tinkers—bunch o' hobos—cloggin' up the public thoroughfare? I understand that most of 'em are on welfare, breedin' like rabbits, an' have never worked a day in their lives. Why doesn't the government just round 'em up and deport 'em? I hear they're all foreigners, Lithuanian or somethin', right?" He said this with a curled lip and disgust one might reserve for an infestation of rats or vermin.

I was used to this vicious stereotype of Ireland's homeless nomads. The locals were the worst perpetrators, blaming the travelers for every calamity, except the weather. But I rarely heard it from tourists, and never with this edge of contempt. It was near the end of the week, and I was already sick of overbearing Yanks, so I wasn't about to let it be. "No, Mr. Cassidy, that's all wrong," I said. "Many of these people are friends of mine; mostly decent, hardworking people who've been handed a tough row to hoe. Their ancestors—all pure Celts, not Lithuanian—were evicted from their homes during the Great Hunger. Could have happened to any of us. They just adapted to the road as a way of life and never settled. They're our fellow citizens, doing the best they can, like all the rest of us."

Cassidy stood up and leaned across the bar in what seemed to be his characteristic sneer: "What is it wid you Irish guys anyway? When are you going to quit pla-yin' the victim? Didn't the Famine happen back in the 1930s or somethin' like that? How about givin' it a rest already?"

I felt the blood rush to my face, anger rising to the point where I had to fight for breath. I turned away from the bar to compose myself, then wheeled back on Cassidy, squaring my full 6´2˝ frame above his beefy face: "Now you listen to me, Mister Cassidy. We're NEVER going to forget what happened back there or 'give it a rest'—as you put it—and I'll tell you why. First, let me set you straight on language and dates: We call it 'The Great Hunger' and it happened in the 1840s, '46-'51, to be pre-cise. And here's the thing: There never was any 'famine' in Ireland, which is, by definition, an absolute shortage of food. You can't have a famine where food is abundant, right? Being exported to feed absentee landlords! It was a deliberate starvation, an attempted genocide by the British, who found us a nuisance, like rodents or roaches, deserving extermination."

Cassidy had backed off, like most bullies, surprised and shaken by my outburst. The redheaded twins and brown-eyed wife exchanged looks, sipping their drinks nervously. I wasn't done. I homed in on Cassidy, leaned across the bar, and upped the ante: "Are you aware that millions of us—*millions!*—starved to death? They damn nearly succeeded in their genocide attempt. But we Celts are a tough crowd, so we survived to tell the tale and to prevail—not as victims, but as proud, free people, who are not about to forget our own history, especially when it's deliberately airbrushed."

Cassidy had backed up toward the door, and I came out from behind the bar, in pursuit, hammering home the point:

"All that garbage about the potato crop failing and millions merrily emigrating to a better life in America, Australia, Canada—pure British propaganda, one of their specialties. Sure, the potato crop failed, but there was enough food in Ireland to not only feed the people, but for export as well. Does that qualify us as victims, Mister Cassidy, or do you think we should have just smiled and invited our genocidal landlords over for tea and crumpets?"

Cassidy rolled his eyes, like a petulant teenager who'd been reprimanded by a parent, and played his lowest default card: "Nice speech, but I don't see how anyone knows for sure about these things. Like you said yourself, it was a long time ago. Might never have happened. I just don't believe in these socialist conspiracy theories. Seems to me just another excuse for welfare queens and moochers—like your buddies, the tinkers—to avoid an honest day's work."

For a moment I was speechless—not believing what I was hearing. I'd heard about holocaust deniers before, but never encountered one up close and personal, like this. I felt ashamed of having let this eejit get to me, and I decided to cut my losses, right there. So I abruptly changed the subject.

"Oh, you were mentioning an interest in the Bolger farm. Seems a long way to come for 20 acres of land. When did you hear about it?"

Cassidy came back from the door, seemingly relieved at the reprieve, and quickly pivoted from denier to buyer. He had a litany of questions. What was land going for around here? Was Bolger's land good quality? Why was it going to public auction, *really?*

I was determined to steer Cassidy away from any land purchase in Rathdangan, let alone Bolger's farm. If he'd been in the Fox & Goose in New York City when he'd run his mouth just now, it might well have been the last time he spoke. I sensed trouble as soon as he'd walked in the door. Now, my job was to be sure he walked out and kept on going.

I didn't need to gild the lily here; the reality of the situation should have been plenty to dissuade any rational prospect. So I gave him the unvarnished truth, including the hostility in the community at Flanagan's ruling and the resolve to boycott the auction, or worse.

I finished with a local conviction, widely shared—one of the few I happened to agree with: "I really don't think anyone will have much luck in that place. If you ask me, it seems cursed. People who never harmed anybody seem to have had no luck there. And I pity any outsider who buys it. Buying that place is signing up for endless hassles and lawsuits, I guarantee it. There are lots of other farms for sale around here, better farms, free and clear. Sure, if I were you, I'd give the Bolger place a wide berth."

Cassidy suddenly snapped back to his bullying form. He took a belligerent step toward me, jamming a stubby index finger into my chest. "Okay, pal," he shouted, "I think I see your little game here. Scare off all the Yanks and outsiders with threats of family disputes and lawsuits; this way, one of your friends—maybe some of your tinker buds—can buy it for a song and slip you a few pounds for your efforts. Do I look that stupid to you?"

I was tempted to take the bait and say: "Yes, indeed you do." Instead, I bit my tongue and stepped behind the bar to gather my thoughts. I wiped off a couple of glasses, then leaned calmly across the bar and said: "Hey, Mister Cassidy, you're going to put whatever spin you want on it. You seem to have a knack for that, but I will tell you this: I'd be more careful how you talk about our ancestors and our people—subjects you clearly know nothing about—in the next pub you visit. Not everyone is going to let insults go with a correction of basic facts, if you get my drift. And I'd like that courtesy to begin right now."

A murderous anger crossed Cassidy's florid face, and his wife, Sarah, put a restraining hand on his arm. She'd seen this look before, and it had undoubtedly ended badly. He shook off her hand roughly, and stood, like a bull about to charge. I braced myself, expecting the worst. Instead, he took a deep breath, perhaps remembering his parole officer's warning, and approached me with the extended finger again.

This time I was ready. I looked him in the eye, put up my hand calmly, and said, "Don't! I wouldn't try that again, if I were you." He looked at his sons for support; they looked away, and he backed off, seeming at a loss for the next move. Then he just stood in the middle of the pub and shouted in a blustery, macho voice:

"Listen, pal, let me tell you somethin'. I don't give a rat's ass about any family dispute or that bullshit you ran by me about bad luck and a curse on the place. Who do you think you're kiddin'? I'm just interested in a good investment for my family, pure and simple. I doubt any of us would ever want to live down here in the boonies anyway, so local popularity is not one of my concerns. But if we like what we see, and the land is for sale by the legal owner—no liens, no nuthin'—we intend to buy it at the auction."

With that, he drained the Guinness and signaled the others to finish up. But he couldn't resist a parting shot, doing a poor imitation of Al Capone sending a message to the Feds: "By the way, if any of the locals don't like my bedside manner, they can stuff it where the sun don't shine. I wasn't a cop in South Bronx for 25 years to be scared of a bunch o' Micks. An' I have my two big Cassidy boys here who can handle themselves, like all the Cassidy clan. We don't go lookin' for no trouble, but God help them that starts up wid us. I say, bring it on, if it ever comes down to that. No problema!"

Cassidy clearly relished the thought of a brawl to protect "his property"—perhaps the first bit of real estate he'd ever been able to imagine calling his own. I worried that my clumsy attempt to steer him away from the auction might have backfired, turning it into an issue of his manhood.

I shrugged, gave him his change and forced a smile: "Hey, no hard feelings, Mr. Cassidy. I was just trying to be helpful, that's all. I like to call it as I see it." I stuck out my hand and he hesitated before offering a stubby fingered, bone-crunching handshake—quickly withdrawn—with no eye contact. I didn't let him see the pain he'd inflicted, but I noticed later that my pinkie was oozing blood where he'd crushed it against my Claddagh ring.

I walked them out and gave them directions to Bolger's farm. We said our awkward goodbyes, and they drove away, Cassidy at the wheel of the new Jag—golf clubs on the roof, temporary plates and a Penn State decal in the back window. The next time I saw Kevin Cassidy, it would be under dramatically different circumstances.

Cassidy's visit left me a bit shaken. The man was definitely bad news, an ignorant lout with no respect for the ancestors, the culture, or for vulnerable, downtrodden people. Here was a man who would willfully pursue the Bolger land just to make a point, tone-deaf to the landmines he was stepping on. How could we have been so unlucky as to have attracted this piece of work, of all people?

The other question raised by his visit was why the auction hadn't been in any of the local papers. Phil and Jimmy Tobin must have figured they'd bypass the locals and entice a wider circle of buyers by advertising only in the *Irish Times*, a cosmopolitan Dublin daily with an international readership. The fact that it was being held at a hotel in Kilkenny, the upscale Kildara Arms, also suggested they wanted to foil any mischief the locals might have in mind to obstruct the auction. No doubt they'd hire a battalion of guards to keep order, just in case the rumors about sabotage had any truth to them.

Finnegan's was jumpin' that night, as news of the auction and my altercation with Cassidy spread. I broke the news to Carby, who just shook his head and smiled before heading for the loo in the back. He didn't come back for about a half hour, so Matt Murphy finally went back there to see if he was all right.

No one commented when they both returned, Matt with a fatherly arm around Carby's shoulder. Paddy Crotty joined them immediately, as did several other regulars, huddling in the corner, whispering, as if in a secret paramilitary conclave drawing up insurgent deployment plans. From the muted tone—so uncharacteristic of those particular individuals—we had little doubt that their target was Jim Tobin's auction at the venerable Kildara Arms.

The auction fell on Tuesday, May 25, 1989. It was a glorious day, the kind we sometimes see in Ireland in late May. Birdsong filled the river vale in a grand harmony—meadowlarks, curlews, blackbirds, thrush, and harriers—echoing up and down the serpentine, meandering Barrow on its way to the Irish Sea. The swallows were back from their warmer climes, darting angels in black-and-white garb, busily anointing the cowsheds and barns, claiming their territory; a quilt of white and yellow daisies flowed down from the Blackstairs, cascading toward the river, their border of purple clover dancing in the spring breeze. Inspired by the rare sunshine and the beauty of the day, I closed Finnegan's—knowing my regulars would all be at the auction in Kilkenny. I drove by the Bolgers' farm on the way and spotted Cassidy's Jaguar parked by the roadside. A small entourage walked slowly around the lower meadows, inspecting the river access. That would be young Jay Tobin, giving Cassidy and other prospective buyers one final walkthrough, just in case they'd missed anything.

I spotted Carby leaning against the stable door, watching his unwanted visitors in the distance, no doubt feeling angry and helpless, reality closing in. As the prospect of a hanging is said to "concentrate the mind," the prospect of eviction from the only home he'd ever known was surely akin to a hanging in Carby's tormented mind. And as Yeats warned us long ago, in the wake of great trespasses against the soul, "A terrible beauty is born." I felt sorry for Carby, wanted to comfort him, somehow, but dared not, fearing his wrath or an accusation of being some kind of accomplice. I never told him that I'd tried to talk Cassidy out of even bidding.

At noon, the tractors began pulling into the circular driveway of the Kildara Arms. Paddy Crotty led the parade, perched on his huge Massey-Ferguson, hauling a large trailer loaded with about a hundred bales of hay. Matt Murphy came next with his ancient McCormick, then Darby Breen, driving his brother's John Deere Harvester, which blocked the entire front entrance. Down the main Kilkenny Road, all the way to the Butler Hotel, tractors of all size and vintage crawled along at a snail's pace, then stalled in gridlock, as did all traffic within ten square blocks of the auction.

The garda arrived in force, too late. They'd been sorting out an accident on the main Dublin Road from earlier that morning. By the time they returned to the station, they had to walk a full ten blocks to get to the hotel and begin directing traffic. Paddy Crotty, first in their line of fire, threw up his hands in mock frustration, shouting, "It's about time yez got here. How's a man supposed to park his chariot with the traffic a feckin' mess. Will yez do somethin' ta sort this out, for Chrissakes?"

Sergeant (Jackie) Terrell—my stalwart teammate for Kilkenny—turned red around his starched collar, glared at Crotty, then pulled out his notebook and started writing down names and license tags. The other two garda looked on passively before Terrell wheeled on them, shouting: "Snap to and get all the names and licenses of this mob. They're gonna live to regret this before I'm done with them." To which Crotty replied, "Mob is it now; and since when is it a crime ta drive a tractor and be stuck in a traffic jam? I'd be careful about yer choice of words if I were you, Sergeant. We'll remember this, trust me. Don't forget who pays yer salary. I'll be sure the chief hears about this when yer next promotion comes up." With that, he winked at Matt Murphy, stepped off the tractor, and pointed toward the foyer of the hotel where the auctions were staged.

By 2 p.m., there was standing room only in the mezzanine ballroom, where the Bolger auction was advertised on large poster boards. The bar had been open all day, so many of the patrons were already in Guinness-fine form, eager for the show to begin. I spotted the square, bald head of Kevin Cassidy, looking dapper in a sports coat and tie, with several other strangers standing up near the front, in ready view of the auctioneer's podium.

At 2:20 p.m., Jimmy Tobin, flanked by two of the young garda, banged his gavel and called the auction to order.

"Good afternoon, ladies and gentlemen. Today, we have here a fine parcel of 20 acres of land at Rathdangan with road and river access. Farmhouse, outbuildings, livestock, and implements will be offered as part of the auction. The land is freehold and is being auctioned as a going concern, under court order: no liens or impediments. The buyer will be required to make a 50% good-faith payment in cash or cashier's cheque at the end of the auction, with the remainder to be paid at the closing."

Tobin glanced around, saw a sea of frothy black Guinness, the milling crowd, and smiled smugly at his audience. So far, so good. This was going to be a breeze.

"Now, do I hear an opening bid on this fine, 20-acre parcel, with river and road access?"

A commotion in the back of the ballroom disrupted his question, as Paddy Crotty and his gang came surging forward. Crotty paused in stride, stood on a chair, surrounded by his disciples, and boomed his best Jehovian declaration: "This auction is illegal, and any sale will be immediately rendered null and void! I speak as a representative of the entire Rathdangan community."

As usual, Crotty had more to say: "We refuse to bid on this land and will block access to any outsider who tries to buy it. If anyone attempts to break this boycott— we will treat them as scabs and pigs, and we'll sue them in a class action suit—taking it all the way to the High Court in Dublin if it comes ta dat!"

Stomping, whistles, and raucous applause drowned out Jimmy Tobin, as he struggled to get the microphone to work, cursing a red-faced hotel employee who'd been sent to the rescue.

Ashen with anger, finally with a working microphone, Tobin homed in on Crotty from his auctioneer's podium:

"Mister Crotty! MISTER CROTTY! YOU ARE OUT OF ORDER! You are interrupting a public auction and seeking to intimidate prospective buyers, which is a felony subject to prosecution and jail time. If you know what's good for you, you will cease this outrageous display at once and vacate the premises. Otherwise, I will have you escorted out by Sergeant Terrell here."

Crotty, embracing the spotlight, smiled and replied: "Sure Mr. Tobin, ya can try to have me removed if ya like. But I speak as an elected official, an' ya'll soon see dat yer out of yer depth here in Kilkenny. So *if ye know what's good for ye*, ye'll go back ta Wexford where ya belong and lave us in peace here. There's no way we'll stand by an' watch some stranger take the bread out of a neighbor's mouth."

Without waiting for Tobin, Sergeant Terrell charged out into the crowd, nightstick in hand, crimson face glowing under the shiny peak of his sergeant's cap. He unceremoniously dragged Crotty from his perch, twisted his arm behind his back, and started frog-marching him out of the ballroom. But the crowd refused to budge, blocking the way, tripping the sergeant, and hanging on Crotty's belt.

The two young garda waded in, but were quickly brushed aside by the surging crowd, now morphing into a howling mob converging on Jimmy Tobin, as he backed toward the side door of the ballroom, a panicked look in his eyes.

That's when all hell broke loose, as Tobin and the garda fled for their lives, the mob in hot pursuit. Like so many well-documented cases in human history, the mob's bloodlust trumped all sense of rationality in a heartbeat, leaving only a raging human beast in pursuit of its hapless prey.

As luck would have it, I escaped the awful orbit of contagion, witnessing it from the safe distance of the mezzanine balcony, from which I now beat a hasty retreat to my car, parked in a vacant lot at the edge of town. I thought Carby would be pleased with the show of support, but I also knew that this was a short-lived, Pyrrhic victory.

It felt more like a botched execution, the prisoner still barely alive, twisting in the wind. It was as if the hangman had been momentarily distracted, yet bound to return to his grizzly task, hood in place, determined to trigger that "terrible beauty" Yeats so prophetically coined in commenting on the Easter Rising of 1916.

Things moved fast from there. After the garda regrouped and dispersed the mob—with a few bashed skulls and four arrests—it seems that Cassidy and two other bidders were invited to a private auction later that evening at Jimmy Tobin's office in Enniscorthy. The other two, merchant farmers from Borris and Gowran, looking for an outfarm, drove up the price after Cassidy made it clear he didn't care about their bids.

He did mention "that asshole bartender's attempt to scare me off…" and that I'd "messed with the wrong guy." All this came out in court, later. The upshot, as I heard it from Paddy Crotty: "Cassidy bought the Bolgers' 20 acres—the very best half, facing the Barrow. Sure he'll have no luck there, as sure as me name is Crotty." For once, and perhaps only this once, Paddy Crotty and I had the exact same sentiment.

Cassidy paid "serious money" up front—we never did find out how much the 20 acres went for—and headed straight for Brendan Cowan's office, a local solicitor in

Enniscorthy that Tobin had recommended. They drew up the settlement papers and closed two days later—Thursday, May 27. The land was now legally the property of Kevin Cassidy & Sons, home address: Bronx, New York, U.S.A. He was legally eligible to buy it because, apparently, his grandfather was from Kilkenny, and Cassidy had filed to become an Irish citizen years before.

I learned this directly from the horse's mouth when the Cassidy men folk stopped by Finnegan's later that day, on their way up to Dublin after the closing. It was mid-afternoon, a slow hour; fortunately—given how their visit played out—no one else was in the pub. Cassidy, pumped with the pride of ownership, had a message for me and the rest of Rathdangan: "Didn't want ya hearin' it secondhand, Myles, my man. Thought you'd like to know, now that we're gonna be neighbors. Surely those assholes on the tractors didn't think that little caper in Kilkenny was gonna scare us off; they must take us for bunch of … whatdya call 'em here? …Feckin' eejits?"

All this with a smirk, the twins standing by like bodyguards, tattooed biceps folded across huge chests, refusing a drink as their da took his time over a pint of Guinness.

Given the atmosphere and what had just transpired in Kilkenny, I had to admit it took some brass for Cassidy to show up at Finnegan's. I certainly wasn't about to take the bait again. "Not a problem, Mr. Cassidy. People around here are decent, law-abiding citizens. No one is going to bother you on your land."

Cassidy looked at me steadily with pale, hostile eyes, crouching forward for effect. "That's good," he growled, "cause as I mentioned already, we can handle ourselves. We just made an investment here an' we'll do what we have to do to protect our property... you can tell that to the wise guys wid the tractors." The twins high-fived each other in solidarity with their da, muttered something, and almost suffocated at another inside joke.

I turned away to hide my quick flush of anger, wiping off glasses behind the bar, before responding: "I don't think so, Mr. Cassidy. Sure you can tell 'em yourself, if the occasion should arise. No point in crossing bridges before you meet them now, is there?" He glared at me for what felt like eternity, started toward me with the finger pointed, thought better of it, then let loose with his mandatory last word: "Yeah, well, I find it's good policy to let wise guys know what's in store for 'em *before* they set foot on any of my bridges. That's all I gotta say for now."

With that, he gulped the last of his stout, tossed me one last "Up yours!" stare, and stalked off without a backward glance, massive bodyguards in tow. Moments later, I heard the Jag peel out of the parking lot, spewing gravel in all directions, heading for the Dublin Road.

The regulars would arrive soon, so I got busy tapping kegs and setting up for the night. I hadn't seen Carby since the auction, and I was getting worried. All the miscreants ("wise guys") were out of jail, had scheduled hearings for "hooliganism"—before, guess who? Judge

Brian Flanagan—and, at Finnegan's, we were treated to a nightly seminar on legal strategies for each case. Not surprisingly, Paddy Crotty, though the ringleader, had not been arrested. I smiled as I imagined the look on Sergeant Terrell's face—Jackie always had trouble with subtlety—as he was advised by Judge Flanagan to show some respect for "Mr. Crotty, our esteemed TD"— Member of Parliament—even if he had been inciting a mob to violence.

The explanation for Carby's absence was probably simple, I thought: He was, no doubt, stretched with the spring planting. After the snowstorm and flooding, a precious month had been lost, and, like the rest of the island, we were a month behind our normal work schedule. Carby was also probably tired of getting advice; advice that had not served him well up to now, advice that was unlikely to abate much in the aftermath of the sale. Knowing him, I just assumed he was in denial that the auction had ever happened, or that, if it had happened, it was of no interest to him. He was probably just getting on with his life as if nothing had changed. That was the Carby I'd always known, up to now.

His absence only stoked the fires of debate at Finnegan's. Everyone had a strong position, of course, all fool-proof—"guaranteed to work," if only Carby had the wisdom to heed their sage advice. He should sue, sue, sue—everyone, it seemed: Molly as executor of the estate for Andy's will, claiming the new will had been made in the face of coercion and mental impairment; Jimmy Tobin for breach of public trust in announcing a public auction only to go and hold a secret one; Cassidy, to block his right-of-way access to the new purchase, since he would have to use the Bolger laneway to enter the land; Cassidy, again, for a government "taking" under the "Land Commission Act of 1945," restricting land ownership to native Irish, or those with Irish residence for at least two years before purchasing more than five acres.

All that litigating fever seemed moot on Saturday morning when a red lorry marked "Ryan Bros, Bagenalstown, Co. Carlow," pulled up outside Finnegan's. The driver was looking for directions to the "Bolgers of Rathdangan" and said he had to deliver a load of fencing stakes and wire. I gave him directions and watched him drive off, imagining what Carby would think, or do, when that big rig came down the lane.

I felt a strange premonition as the lorry's tail lights blinked out of sight—that I should have warned the driver of being in danger. But I quickly dismissed it. I had a job to do and no one else to staff the pub, so I just moped back inside, feeling like one of those heavy, black clouds hovering over the Blackstairs Range.

An hour later, Molly Bolger crashed through the door of the pub, tears streaming down her face, sobbing hysterically: "Oh, Myles, Myles, you've got to help me," she blurted. "It's Patrick, he's taken Noel, said he'll kill him unless I write the letter… called me a whore and other awful names... said I'd caused all his troubles... that I'd cost him a fortune. I came straight here because he's always thought well of you, once told me you're the only one who's ever shown him any respect. I didn't... I didn't know where else to turn. Will you help me, please? Oh, please!" She fell to her knees on the hardwood floor, face in her hands, disconsolate—her voice falling off in a pitiful wail.

I reached down and gently helped her to her feet, then took her lovely face in both my hands. "Molly," I said, "Now listen to me, we've got to find Carby. Where do you think he's taken Noel?" I'd read about the mind-set of hostage-takers and the danger of threatening or crowding them.

She looked at me through tormented eyes, now more red than blue, and said, "He told me he'd be at the farm when I was ready to write that letter, that I'd better not call the garda. Kept repeating: 'If ya ever want ta see yer little bastard alive...' Oh, Myles, if anything happens to Noel, I'll never forgive myself." With that, she broke down again, but I'd already ripped off the apron and was writing a note: "Closed. Back at 6 p.m." I stuck it on the front door and we piled into Molly's Morris Minor, with me at the wheel. In no time flat we were zooming out of Rathdangan, speed limits be damned, determined to reach the Bolgers' farm before the worst happened.

A few miles down the road, I heard the whine of a garda's siren coming over the rise behind us, blue lights flashing, and cursed my lousy luck. "Oh, shite!" I fumed, "what are these feckin' eejits doing out here on a Saturday morning?" I pulled over, and Molly started rooting frantically in the glove compartment for her registration. But to our amazement, the garda's car flew past us, immediately followed by another, with a fire truck bringing up the rear. Could someone else have sounded the alarm already? But who? And how could they have known about the kidnapping, since Molly hadn't reported it? Surely, this could not be a coincidence, I thought.

We were about ten kilometers from the farm, so Molly, now a bit calmer, filled me in on the details while I drove.

The previous night, Carby had stopped by her apartment around suppertime, a first since she'd moved there. He announced his mission abruptly, ignoring her offer of tea. "I want ya to write a letter," Carby had demanded, "saying that Da was out o' his mind and that the will is illegal. There's more ta dis t'ing than meets the eye, but I can't tell ya about all dat now. But no way can dat sale ta da Yank stand. Ya gotta write dat letter."

Molly had refused, saying it would be a felony to perjure herself, pointing out that her word wouldn't matter anyway, since there were independent witnesses to the will.

Carby lost it at that point, upsetting the baby, and she'd asked him to leave. He did, but not before a string of threats and the usual choice epithets. "Whore, greedy trollop, bastard," before storming out. She'd considered calling the garda, thought better of it, and tried to sleep, without success.

In the morning, just as she was coming down the stairs on her way to the garda station, she'd met "Patrick" coming up, with a huge suitcase, which he'd carried with one- handed ease. He'd smiled pleasantly and said, "I have a present for you. Let me show you." Inside the apartment, he'd asked her if she'd changed her mind. "Patrick, were you not listening?" Molly answered, "I'm never going to change my mind and become a felon. Are you crazy? There's no point to this. You have to get off this thing and move on. What's done is done."

He paused, took a deep breath, then whipped open the suitcase and pulled out a sawed-off shotgun, pointed it at her head, and scooped up Noel roughly with his free hand. "We'll see about that," he said flatly. "There's more dan wan way ta skin a cat, as da always used ta say." He tossed the shrieking toddler roughly into the suitcase, closed it, and backed out the door holding it like any piece of luggage. Molly could hear Noel's muffled screams as Carby backed down the stairs, gun still pointing in her direction.

Her pleas of, "All right, please! Please! For God's sake, Patrick. I'll do whatever you want. Just don't harm my baby," fell on deaf ears.

Before stepping into the street, he'd paused to issue one final threat: "If ya call the garda, ye'll never see this little bastard of yours agin. Dere's no going back now. Dis is for keeps. Up ta you. I'll be at the farm when yer ready to do business. An' don't bring any company." She'd waited for a few minutes, not wanting to anger him further, before peering out in time to see Carby in his tattered tweed jacket, driving away on the tractor, the suitcase precariously straddling the tow bar.

That's when she dashed for Finnegan's.

"Molly," I said, as she finished the nightmarish account, "know what I think?"

"No, Myles, what?" she said in a despairing whisper that was excruciating to hear.

"I think that Carby's not capable of hurting a fly. This is all bluster, his way of getting back at you for his lost cause. I'm absolutely sure he won't hurt the young lad— that's just not who he is. Trust me, we're going to get Noel back and all will be well in the end."

I finished this assurance just as we turned off the Dublin Road, a four-lane highway, onto the one-lane boreen leading down to the Bolgers' farm. The lush brambles narrowed the lane to less than a car width, and I felt an acute sense of claustrophobia as the thorny branches closed in on the Morris Minor from both sides. Coming around the second bend, I saw the garda's flashers and suddenly felt a lot less confident than I'd been a moment ago.

The laneway was cordoned off with yellow police tape and a large sign warned: "Garda! Keep out!" Ignoring the sign, we raced down the lane in time to hear the opening salvo and see that a group of locals had also converged on the scene: like us, ignoring the warning and the yellow garda cordon.

Speaking forcefully on the bullhorn, my old friend, Sergeant Jackie Terrell, was addressing the farmhouse: "Carby, listen here! This is Sergeant Terrell. I know you don't want to do any harm to yourself or anyone else, so why don't you come out and we can settle this thing peacefully before anyone gets hurt? You're only going to make it harder on yourself holding out like this. Just put your hands where we can see them and come on out!"

Carby's response was instantaneous: An exploding shower of glass from the kitchen window, jabbed by the ugly, sawed-off shotgun. A small team of uniformed garda had been assembled, all armed with high-powered rifles—but under strict orders from Terrell, they held their fire.

Then came Carby's strangled voice, echoing in delayed cadence across the farmyard, "I don't give a shite about harm. HARM! Wasn't it yous that served all dem summons; wasn't it yous dat let the auction go ahead? It's way too late ta talk ta me about harm. Yez can all go ta hell."

Terrell, always tenacious as a bulldog, tried again, bullhorn on full volume: "Carby, tell me what you want us to do. There's no point in this standoff unless you want somethin'. Just ask. I'll see what I can do. I give you my word, as God is my witness. I just can't have you holed up in there threatenin' to kill the garda, yourself, an' God knows who else. Let's be reasonable here."

This time, Carby didn't answer. We just saw the shotgun withdraw from the window. Then silence.

Terrell tried a few more times, with the same result. Finally, after a brief consultation with his team, he gave up and went back to pacing up and down, considering his next move.

Seizing on the lull, I left Molly, walked up to the uniformed huddle, and nonchalantly addressed my friend, Sergeant Terrell, "What's all the fuss about? One would think this was the O.K. Corral."

Jackie smiled weakly. "Seems that Carby pulled a shotgun on Ryan's lorry driver, blocked his access to the farmyard, and ran him off. Cassidy called us out to escort the lorry in, and now Carby is holed up in the farmhouse, threatening to kill Cassidy—an' us—if we come any closer. I think he's gone berserk. Officer O'Toole thinks he heard a baby crying in there as well." Terrell threw up his hands in a gesture of hopelessness. "It's a mess, Myles. You and Molly better get back behind the cordon line for your own safety."

I looked at Terrell and saw an opening, "Oh, that baby you heard? Sure, Carby is babysitting Molly's young lad, Noel, while she went to the shops. She dropped him off out here this morning. She does every Saturday. Loves to play with the dogs now that he can boot around and hold his own."

Terrell looked at me in disbelief and said, "You mean to tell me there's a toddler in there in the middle of all this? Is Bolger nuts or what? God, this thing is a bigger mess than I thought! Myles, just get back, will ya, while I sort this thing? This changes everything." As he said this, he gestured to the young garda, Michael O'Toole, to escort Molly and me behind the yellow line.

I drew Molly aside. "Did you hear that?" I said, sounding my cheerful best. "O'Toole heard Noel inside—he's okay. Listen, I just told Terrell that Carby was baby-sitting Noel, so they don't know what he did. Yet. That could draw a life sentence, you know—so you may not want to make a liar out o' me. I think we can work this out if we can just keep our cool. I think I can talk Carby down, convince him this is a really bad idea. As you said, I think he trusts me, so maybe I can make a move."

She looked at me and said: "Do or say whatever you think will get Noel out safely. That's all I care about. Please God, don't let anything happen to Noel. He's just a baby…" She trailed off, lost in tears and terror.

I gave her a reassuring hug, and thought: "What must be coursing through your mind!"—the baby snatched away by her brother, now gone mad. Looking at the blonde hair and terror-stricken eyes, I realized, perhaps for the first time, that I'd do anything for this woman; *anything*, if it would save her child and relieve her suffering.

I took off my jacket, handed it to her, and said, "Wait here! Don't talk to anyone or say a word about Noel till I get back." I squeezed her shoulder for reassurance and said, "Trust me!" Then I ducked under the yellow tape and jogged down to where Sergeant Terrell was huddled with his team. I spotted Cassidy parked by the barn, sitting in his Jag, taking in the action. I nodded to him curtly as I jogged by, but he just scowled and turned away.

"Hey, Jackie, can I speak to you privately for a minute?" I said this quietly, so that only Terrell could hear me.

"Listen, I have an idea. I know Carby well, and I'm pretty sure he trusts me. As you know, we go way back, and I know he'll talk to me. I can calm things down and keep him from doing any harm to himself or anyone else. I know for sure he won't harm me. We've never had a sour word in our lives." As I said this, I recalled Carby's diatribe the night I refused him whiskey at Finnegan's. I could only hope he'd known it had been for his own good.

Terrell turned away, deep in thought, then wheeled back. "All right, Myles," he said breezily, "I'm only allowing this because you're respected around here, so don't make me regret this decision. Got that?" I nodded and walked toward the farmhouse, my hands out in front where Carby could see them.

Walking up the gravel path, I could almost hear my own heartbeat as I got closer to the broken kitchen window. Far from what I was feeling, I managed to speak in a calm tone of voice.

"Hey Carby, it's Myles. Can I come in so that we can talk this over? I know you don't trust the garda, but I'll give you my word, I don't want to do anything but hear your side of the story."

I could hear Noel clearly, shrieking and laughing joy-fully, as I'd seen him when he was bouncing in Molly's knapsack. I waited for a moment, then tried again.

"Carby? Can you hear me? It's Myles Dunne. May I come in, please? Just wanna chat."

The door opened a crack and the sawed-off shotgun poked out, straight at my chest. Carby spoke hoarsely from behind the door, almost in a whisper. "Come in, Myles," he said, "I don't have anything ta say, but sure we might as well have a pint, for auld times sake. Lord knows, I owe ya a few."

I stepped gingerly into the dim kitchen and was in-stantly assaulted by the familiar stench of rotten eggs.

Carby sounded like the upbeat guy I'd known for the last few months at Finnegan's, but the shotgun was still pointed at me. I casually walked over to him, gently pressed the barrel downward, and said, in a steady voice: "Will you put that thing away before you get us both in trouble? Didn't your da teach you to never point a gun at anyone unless you intend to use it?"

He laughed, propped the gun against the dresser, and said: "Ah sure, the damn thing isn't even loaded. I haven't had a cartridge in it for years. Doubt it even works anymore." We both laughed out loud then, me in relief, Carby at the joke of the impotent gun, I'd imagined.

He moved toward the oak cupboard, took out two bottles of Guinness, popped the caps, handed me one, and toasted me with his own. "Up Kilkenny," he said, as if we were back in Finnegan's, "Here's to those six championships, Myles. Jaysus, you were a great wan. I think we're gonna win it agin dis year. Whatdeya t'ink?" I took a sip of the stout, raised the bottle toward him and said, "Hope so, Carby. The lads have been working awful hard."

The scene in the kitchen was right out of Dickens. Noel was naked, running around the filthy concrete floor, face black as a coal-miner, babbling, "Doggie, Doggie," with great delight to his pals, two plump border collie puppies. Like three canine littermates, they were playing tug-o'-war with a rag doll, the pups snarling and acting fierce. A bowl of milk stood in the middle of the floor; beside it, a half-full quart bottle with a teat on the end, normally used to feed calves. The black-and-white puppies, not yet housebroken, had peed all over the concrete floor, which had been decorated with jam jar circles before setting—a common flourish in rural kitchens—the perfect catchment for a puppy loo.

Carby pointed toward the animal scrum and smiled. "The young lad is great craic," he said, "I've got to be careful not to get too attached. I s'pose she'll be wantin' 'im back soon enough."

I reached down and extracted Noel from the pack, much to the puppies' distress. "Yeah, Carby," I nodded in solemn agreement, "I think that's a safe bet. What the hell were you thinking, anyway, when you went into town and took him? Why didn't you come out and talk to me? I could've helped you out. You know we're all in your corner." As I said this, I walked over to a water bucket by the stove, wet a kitchen towel and started cleaning Noel's sooty face, expecting a fuss.

Instead, he seemed to like it, laughing and poking me in the face with his filthy little fingers, saying: "Da, da," repeatedly. I smiled wistfully. "Sorry son," I whispered, "I only wish…" and tickled his tummy before wrapping him in a towel as a makeshift diaper. This was one charismatic youngster, I thought, the kind adults instantly fall in love with and vie for their attention. I already felt myself under his spell as I cradled him in my left arm and offered him the quart bottle, which he ravenously devoured.

"Carby," I said in a deeply earnest tone, "I don't know what it is you want or why you took the young lad. But I do know this: It's wrong to keep a child from his mother, and I intend to bring him out there and give him back. Once he's safe, I promise you I'll come back and I'll stand up for you, for whatever you want."

He looked at me with those sad, black eyes and said: "Myles, sure I don't know what da fuck I'm doing. Yer right. I've gotta figure some other way outa dis mess I got meself into."

I washed the soot off my own face, too, in preparation for leaving, and said, "Well, think about it—what you actually want, I mean. You haven't done anything wrong yet, really. I told Terrell you were baby-sitting the young lad for Molly, so you're still okay. Now I'm going out there, and I want you to stay put. Don't move a muscle till I get back, and for Chrissakes keep that feckin' shotgun out o' sight!"

Carby was still nursing the Guinness, an old habit, I thought. I stood up, holding Noel, who was beginning to squirm, crying, "I want my mammy," over and over. I wrapped him in a curtain from the kitchen shelf, rocked him gently, and whispered, "It's okay, *son*, you'll have your mammy in a minute. She's waiting for you outside, and she's gonna buy you all the sweets you can eat today. How does that sound?" He smiled for a split second, buried his head in my chest, and sobbed softly.

I looked at the two puppies, now barking furiously at all the attention their two-legged playmate was getting. Suddenly I had an idea. "Carby, can I buy one of the pups—a present for Noel? Looks to me like they're great chums, and you don't need two borders."

Without hesitation, Carby picked up the big male, clearly the alpha of the litter, and handed him to Noel. "Here, he can have 'im. It's on the house. Like ya said, it's a present ta me nephew." He smiled his crooked little smile and bent to console the remaining puppy.

I headed for the door, Noel cradled in my left arm, the big border pup under the other. I paused before stepping out and said, "Carby, remember what I told you. Stay cool till I get back. Don't go near the window—they have some sharpshooters out there and you'll be a sitting duck without me. Got it? I'll be right back." Carby nodded, fear in his eyes, like a confused little boy afraid of being left alone.

I stepped out with my two sidekicks, Noel shyly hiding his face, the border wriggling ferociously. I hurried down the gravel path, smiling at the thought of Molly's face when she saw Noel. Sergeant Terrell came to meet me, Officer O'Toole restraining Molly from charging forward.

I spoke to Terrell quietly, and he reached out to help me carry the sturdy border. "Listen, Jackie, I got to get back in there right away. I promised Carby. He's ready to come out, no conditions or anything. He's just confused and scared, so call off your men. He's not even armed— the gun's useless. Just give 'em a bit of space, OK?"

"Okay, Myles," Terrell replied. "I'm playin' it your way for now. So far, so good."

I dashed past him, saw Molly running toward us, and I'll never forget the expression in her eyes—some exquisite blend of grief, relief, and love. I handed Noel over, and he clung to her like a monkey, sobbing and laughing at the same time, sounds she lavishly reciprocated. The toddler chanted, "Mammy, mammy, mammy" and Molly cooed, "Oh, my baby! My baby!" It was a litany of joyful mysteries.

Finally, she looked up and met my gaze. "I'll never know how to thank you…" She couldn't finish, and I turned away, blushing. I quickly focused on Terrell and the pup, explaining loudly so that all could hear, that this was a present from Carby to his nephew, and that all the puppy needed was to be housebroken.

I asked Terrell for a favor—if he'd be sure young O'Toole drove Molly and Noel home safely right away? I gave Molly a soft pat on the arm and turned back to Carby and the farmhouse. I should have been relieved, but I wasn't.

As I started back up the gravel walkway, Carby opened the door and stepped out. He was holding the smaller border collie pup in one hand, and, to my horror, the useless shotgun in the other. I bolted forward. "Carby," I shouted, "Drop the gun! Drop the damn gun!" That's when I heard the first shot, coming from the right, by the barn.

Carby dropped like a statue to the gravel, blood gushing from his temple. The puppy howled in agony and scurried sideways toward the house, looking hurt in the hindquarters. I ran forward, yelling, "Carby, you goddamn fool! Didn't I tell you to stay in the house? What the hell were you...?"

I never heard the second shot, only felt a sharp stab in my lower back before the world went black.

I woke in St. Luke's General Hospital in Kilkenny two days later. I was in the ICU, and the nurse in charge, Sheila, told me some of the story. I'd been shot in the back with a high-powered deer rifle, a Remington, she'd heard. It was not a kind used by any of the garda. They'd arrested a suspect. She said the garda had been around to talk to me, but the doctors wouldn't allow it. Not yet. She, in turn, was under strict orders not to discuss any other details of the shooting, with me or anyone else, except what she'd already shared.

The bullet had missed my spinal cord, but shattered two vertebrae in my lower back. "You're a very lucky man," she said, "another millimeter and you'd have been a paraplegic for sure. As it stands, there's a good chance you'll walk again, perhaps a full recovery, with time."

The following morning, Dr. Brosnihan, the young surgeon, came in on his rounds to tell me about the emergency procedure that had saved my life. It took his team six hours, racing against the clock. I marveled at his youthful face—he couldn't have been a day over thirty—as he told me all this, proud of his accomplishment, and, as a raving Kilkenny hurling fan, happy to make a save for the cause.

About to leave, he turned back and said, "Oh, Myles, I'm sorry to tell you this…" He hesitated, took a deep breath and said, "Your friend Carby didn't have such good luck. He's alive, but the long-term prognosis is not good, a permanent vegetative state—known as PVS. Really tragic. He's on life support over in the north wing."

Molly came in later. She was wearing the dark blue dress and yellow scarf—same as she'd worn to the first hearing—holding a large bunch of deep-purple lilacs. At first I thought I was hallucinating from the morphine—this blonde, angelic apparition at my bedside—until she spoke. "Myles! Oh, Myles, thank God you're alive. I thought we'd lost you, too. You have no idea how..." She broke off as Sheila strode in to check my blood pressure and give me my meds.

Sheila withdrew, with a mumbled warning about my needing rest. Molly pulled up a chair and took my right hand in both of hers. Her distinctive perfume blended with the lilacs from across the room. I sensed her pulse through the warmth of those strong hands, and felt a sudden rush of pure ecstasy. I could vaguely hear the traffic whizzing by on Main Street and the deep bass voice of a TV anchor from the nurses' station down the hall.

Without warning, I burst into tears, embarrassing both of us.

I was so grateful to be alive, so happy to see Molly, to feel her perfumed presence. I swiped at the tears awkwardly with the back of my free hand, before she took out her lace handkerchief and gently wiped them away. Then she smiled, lighting up the room with those azure-blue eyes, saying: "There! I'll bet you feel a lot better. We could all stand a good cry right now." I just smiled weakly, and inquired about the carnage back at the farm.

She sat on the edge of the spare bed and told me the whole story, in no particular sequence. How Kevin Cassidy had the high-powered Remington in the back of the Jag. How he'd gloated when he thought Carby and I were both dead, something about teaching us to "mess with" the Cassidys. How he was handcuffed by Sergeant Tyrrell, Cassidy protesting self-defense, as he was taken to the county jail in Kilkenny, where he was now awaiting trial. No bail allowed; flight risk too great. How Patrick, miraculously still alive, and I had been rushed to St. Luke's by ambulance from Goresbridge.

What she didn't tell me, and I had to hear from Sheila later, was that she'd actually saved both our lives. Molly had witnessed the shooting just as she and Noel were being ushered off the site by the garda. But for her professional calm and well-placed tourniquets, we'd both have bled out before the emergency medical technicians (EMTs) arrived from Kilkenny—an interminable 90 minutes later.

She also didn't tell me what Dr. Broshihan had just confided about Carby. Perhaps she knew something I didn't, held out some hope for her brother, or was waiting for a prayer to be answered? When Sheila came back to end the visit and give me an injection, Molly rose, gave me a peck on the cheek, and promised to be back "soon."

Sheila showed me the blaring headline in the *Irish Times* from the shooting: "Taking a Stand for the Land: Shooting in Rathdangan Dispute." The news piece, covering two full pages—including photos of the farm, Carby, and mug shots of Cassidy—detailed the back story of the disputed auction, Cassidy's reputation as a "dirty" cop in South Bronx, New York, his history of repeat suspensions for assaults on minorities, and for allegedly taking bribes. He'd finally been fired from the police force, after killing an unarmed teenager who refused a body search. But, curiously, Cassidy was never convicted of anything. As if by magic, the case had just evaporated, no trace to be found in the public record.

A month after Cassidy shot us, I was transferred to Plunkett Rehab Center, still in the wheelchair, but with a promising prognosis. It might be a year, two years—no one could say with any degree of precision. But I would be able to walk, run, and even play hurling again. Dr. Brosnihan was ebullient, assuring me with great confidence that I'd make a full recovery and resume my role as player/coach with the Kilkenny senior team.

My surrogate parents, Uncle Tommy and Aunt Margaret, came to help move me to rehab. They'd hired a stand-in at Finnegan's, assuring me my job was safe: "Waiting for you when yer ready to come back." I didn't have the heart to tell them that I had other plans.

Carby languished for another month on life support. Then, one night, his heart just stopped beating. Mercifully. The night nurse found him on her rounds with a peaceful look on his face. Molly came by to tell me the news. "Patrick passed away in his sleep last night," was all she said.

She looked drawn and pale, but also relieved, I thought. I saw the news as a mixed blessing, knowing she was now free to go, free of all the obligations that had chained her loyal heart to Rathdangan for so long. But I also knew what it meant for us, and for that I had no words to capture the dread.

Over the past month, she'd come by to see me every day after she'd stopped in to hold her brother's hand for a few minutes and read to him in the ICU. She told me that there was scientific evidence that even PVS victims were soothed by the human touch and could recognize familiar voices.

Sometimes, to my delight, she'd stay until the end of visiting hours, filling me in on all the news that I was missing at Finnegan's. Other times, she'd just breeze in, dropping a little gift of flowers or chocolate before dashing off. But she'd always leave me with some gesture of affection: a peck on the cheek, a pat on the arm, a squeeze of the hand. This was the best part of my day: the smell of her perfume, the azure eyes, golden hair, soft lips—pure, heavenly, healing balm. Ecstasy. It was what I dreamed of, lived for, and woke up for each morning. It was the wellspring of my determination to get up and get moving again.

Now she'd be going away, to San Francisco, out of my life. I'd probably never see her again. What did I have to live for without her? And yet, there was no way I could burden her with yet another millstone in Rathdangan. She deserved better than this squintin' window village could ever offer, certainly more than my current prospects could promise.

I broached the subject first: "Well, I suppose you'll be heading for San Fran as soon as the funeral's over? I'm sure you can't wait to see the end of this place after all that's happened."

She looked out the window for a long time without answering, then turned and pulled up the chair, as usual, her eyes holding mine. "Listen, Myles," she said, speaking slowly, "I didn't tell you, but I've made a commitment for two years to Kilkenny General, as director of their Public Health Service. I didn't know how long Patrick might linger—it could have been years—but I had this opportunity, and I didn't want to let it slip away."

As she said this, she smiled gently, leaned forward, put her arms around my neck, and gave me a long, soulful kiss. She drew back, blue eyes glistening, and said, "I got tired of waiting for you to kiss me; sure, someone has to make a move around here. You know what they say, Myles: 'Only the brave deserve the fair!'"

With that, she slid out the door, tossing me a flirtatious smile and a "See you tomorrow, Mr. Dunne" over her shoulder.

All my stoic resolutions flew out the window. I was instantly, deliriously, *crazily* in love. I shouted for joy, "Oh, YES! Oh, YES! There is a God, after all! Thank you, Jesus..." scaring the nurses, who rushed in to see what was up. They were too late; I was no longer there. I was busy flying my trusty Harley Davidson over the Blackstairs Mountains, roaring past the windswept

Nine Stones on Mount Leinster, gunning the engine down through the lush meadows of County Wexford, gliding along the banks of the rushing whitecaps on the storied River Slaney, Molly's arms knotted around my waist, her blonde hair flying in the wind, the sun burning molten in a cloudless sky. I felt an exultant freedom, like an eagle riding the updraft, the wheelchair a distant memory.

Sheila's familiar voice cut across my fantasy. "Mr. Dunne! Mr. Dunne? Are you all right?" she said, sounding alarmed. "There's a woman, a reporter, here from *Irish Magazine*; says it's about an interview you agreed to… about your new novel? I can just tell her you're not feeling up to it, if you wish."

"Oh, that's fine, Sheila," I replied, "I'll be delighted to see her. I'm never too tired to talk about Wolfe Tone and Irish revolutionary heroes."

The arrival of the reporter reminded me of Cassidy's trial, which had opened the same week I started rehab. Just as we'd hoped, they threw the book at Cassidy in Kilkenny circuit court—where the trial was moved at the request of his defense counsel. Cassidy's mouth proved to be his worst enemy—he bragged to Sergeant Terrell of his NRA (National Rifle Association) membership in the U.S. and his special forces training as a sniper in Vietnam.

I'd testified to Carby's death and my own trauma at Rathdangan. Molly and several garda, including Sergeant Terrell, testified to witnessing the shootings. The Irish courts take a dim view of gun-toting vigilantes—whatever their ideology or rationale. For Cassidy, his luck finally ran out.

The jury took less than a half hour to reach a verdict. Guilty on all counts: first degree murder with malice aforethought, reckless endangerment with intent to harm, and illegal use of a firearm. He'd had no license for the Remington.

The jury had yet to announce any awards in the case; that was still under consideration, as was Cassidy's sentence. The prosecutor had asked for life without parole. We didn't really care, as long as it was severe and would take Kevin Cassidy out of circulation for a long time.

It was no surprise that Cassidy also turned out to be bankrupt. Unable to secure the financing for the Bolgers' parcel, the deal fell through, and all 20 acres reverted to Molly and Noel, one more time. This boy was not only charismatic, he was also one of the luckiest youngsters on the planet, as fortune continued to smile on him from the unlikely bowels of that rocky Rathdangan farm.

A few weeks after the trial, just as we thought Rathdangan might return to some degree of normalcy, Molly came by Plunkett Rehab in a whirl of excitement. I was now able to abandon the wheelchair most of the time, having graduated to a cane with the help of their gifted, compassionate physical therapists. She'd brought my favorite Chinese take-out, beef with broccoli, and a story that, even now, may still be a fairy tale.

"Myles, you're not going to believe this," she began, as we started to eat, "but something incredible has just happened."

I swallowed my first bite of beef, smiled, and said, "Let me guess! Cassidy's been sentenced to life, and the jury awarded you a million pounds for pain and emotional distress."

"Close, Mr. Dunne," she replied, with feigned formality, "but no cigar. It's much better than that."

"OK," I said, "I give up. The suspense is killing me."

Then she told me this remarkable story. The previous evening, a black Mercedes pulled up outside Finnegan's with a German "MD" vanity plate. The driver was one Herman Metzger, Managing Director of Helmholz Industries, a multinational mining company headquartered in Munich, with offices in every major city in Europe and North America. He'd read about Carby's murder and was enquiring for the executor of "The Bolger Estate in Rathdangan." Billy Sullivan, the new bartender, had directed him to Molly's apartment in Goresbridge.

It seemed that just over a year ago, during the previous October, a man named Patrick Bolger contacted

Metzger's firm with a surprising business proposition. Metzger's chauffeur drove down and picked Carby up at Rathdangan crossroads, and the company's executives hosted him for a day at their Irish headquarters in Dublin, talking through the exciting proposition and its potential.

Mr. Metzger had dropped Carby back at the crossroads later that night, and had recalled that "Mr. Bolger promised he'd be in touch once he got a few things sorted. But we never heard back from him. Very disappointing. Thought he might have changed his mind, and we were not at liberty to pursue it any further."

Molly told me the story as you might tell a fairy tale to a child, with a complete sense of wonder, and disbelief—especially at Metzger's account of Patrick's business savvy. Several years earlier, while their father, Andy—the legal owner of the Bolgers' farm at the time—was still alive, Carby and Andy had discretely registered all Rathdangan farm with the Land Commission for a mining license.

The fact that Andy had participated in the registration and applied for a mining license made his decision to cut Carby out of his will all the more cruel and inexplicable.

The successful license was issued in Andy's name after years of deposit sampling from Rathdangan farm—with support from the Land Commission's geologists on how to extract ore samples and apply sulfuric acid "assays" to test their potential. This explained the sulfur dioxide (rotten egg) body odor from Carby, as well as the kitchen stench I detected before the shooting, but it also did something more important: It demonstrated to the satisfaction of the skeptical Department of Mines and mining executives that the Bolgers' farm had rich veins of lead-silver ore, copper, and gold—potentially worth millions, perhaps untold fortunes.

Most amazing of all was Carby's foresight in retaining a legal specialist in mining. How he'd managed to do this and keep it under wraps in Rathdangan is anybody's guess. But one thing was clear: There was no shortage of grey matter under that greasy little cap. Following the legal advice, and assuming he was the heir apparent, Carby had prompted his father to register the whole farm with the Land Commission as a "Protected Private Mining Property," a special designation that retained ownership of the mineral rights with the *original licensee, regardless of who had title to the land.* In short, even if Cassidy had legally purchased all of Bolger's forty acres, the mineral rights would still have belonged to Andy Bolger, and hence to his designated beneficiary—in this case his grandson, Noel. The boy was now literally heir to a gold mine, along with a vast reserve of other precious minerals, *in perpetuity*—"a quare long time," as Darby Breen had reminded us in one of his lectures at Finnegan's.

Watching Molly's gentle face as she related all this, it was clear to me that she still didn't think this was real. What was all too real was the loss of her brother and the grief she felt at his tragic death.

"Well," I said, trying to sound cheerful, "congratulations! This makes you rich as Croesus, a fellow mining mogul, free to rule over your Kilkenny lands as madam's heart desires. It'll certainly give the squintin' window crowd something to talk about."

She smiled wistfully and said, "Croesus, how did you know? Captures exactly how I feel. Oh, the squintin' window is way ahead of you. Especially since I've made no secret of you and me. They already have you pegged as a fortune hunter, although neither of us had any clue whatsoever. Sure, some things are never going to change; you know that, love."

"Indeed I do," I said, "especially if it's within shouting distance of Rathdangan."

While I was happy for her, I was already worrying about what this would do to us. Knowing Molly, it wouldn't have surprised me if she gave it all away to some cause—a homeless shelter or famine relief program in Africa. I half-hoped she would, knowing what wealth can do to people. But I'd never known Molly to be materialistic or extravagant, even when she'd been a well-paid professional living in London. So I dismissed the concern and decided to will myself to be pleased for her and Noel.

"That's all we know for now," she said. "The Land Commission and Phil Shea have to sort all this stuff out. It may take years in the courts. I can't be bothered about all that. I have a job to do, a son to raise, and a man to love—what more could any woman want?"

"Well," I replied, with my arm around her waist, "She might want a man who is able to keep up with Noel and his younger brothers and sisters; who can teach them how to fish, dance, and hurl; and who can still find time to crank out a few good books along the way."

"I like the sound of that," she said, reaching for her coat. "But you've got to walk before you run. Just a bit more patience, my love." Before leaving, she put both arms around my neck and left me with a kiss that would last till next time.

Alone, I reflected on recent events, on my own pot of gold at rainbow's end—Molly—and how little this news mattered. What mattered now was that I would have the courage to earn her love as a man—to go beyond any All-Ireland Championship I'd ever won—and forge a new life from the smithy of this purgatory we'd just survived.

In time, the mining issues would get sorted out. Or not. I was not about to let this sideshow have any standing in my resolve to get my health back, build a life with Molly and Noel, master my writing craft, and make a decent living—enough to support my family, one not beholden to any Land Commission bureaucrat or other crap-shoot that fortune might roll our way.

I was discharged from Plunkett Rehab on a glorious September afternoon. Morning showers had turned to sunshine, and from my window in the rehab I could see the red and green Massy-Ferguson harvesters working the golden wheat fields in the distance, spitting out the white, packaged bales and canvas bags of grain, as if by a giant pair of hands. A flock of wild geese flew in V-formation down the Barrow line, small dots following the river south, their anxious honks calling to me, reminding me that I was about to reenter the universe, alive and well.

Molly had called ahead to alert me: "Hello love, I can't wait to see you. Hope you're up for the dinner party tonight. Paddy Crotty and Joan just wouldn't take no for an answer. They've booked at Mount Juliet, party of 25. You're going to need a jacket and tie; there's a dress code there. They're fairly snooty at the golf club, as you may recall. Tommy and Margaret are baby-sitting Noel; he loves to hear Tommy play the guitar, and Margaret tells him endless bedtime stories, which he seems to understand."

"Mount Juliet! Wow! Dress code, no less? Not to worry. I've got it covered." I said this offhandedly, because it was true. Uncle Tommy—always in my corner—had tipped me off and bought me the proper attire. I needed just one touch to complete the picture. Leaning slightly on my new cane, I walked gingerly across the street to Doyle's Florist, selected a bouquet of twelve red roses, and waited for my sweetheart to arrive.

She stepped out of the Morris Minor two blocks down, reached back for Noel, and popped him fluidly into the backpack. She was wearing a Kelly green dress, which clung to her body in the autumn wind, blonde hair swirling, blue eyes dancing as she navigated the traffic, striding toward me, long legs closing the distance.

She crossed the street, moving gracefully, like a swan gliding across a lake. Noel pointed at the sky, shouting, "Mammy, Mammy, gooses!" I could hear him two blocks away, as if on an amped-up microphone.

"Only the brave deserve the fair." That was my singular thought as she reached for the roses, her other arm caressing my neck, pulling me close. Not to be outdone, Noel lurched forward in his backpack, grabbed my left ear with his sticky little fingers, and shrieked with delight at the capture.

This was how our story would begin. Right here, right now. Once upon a time in Rathdangan…

I liked our chances.

# Acknowledgments

IT'S TRUE THAT WRITING IS a lonely craft, but no book sees the light of day without a host of unsung teachers, mentors, critics, and significant others who've made their unique contribution.

I first want to thank my teacher and mentor at The Iowa Writers' Workshop, Wayne Johnson, for both his inspirational teaching and insightful critiques at every step of the way.

I would also like to acknowledge Professors Conor Ward and Anthony Cunningham, emeritus icons at University College, Dublin, for arranging that Visiting Professorship years ago, allowing me to become reacquainted with my rural Irish roots in a way that made Carby's Fate possible.

Thanks also to Ernest Hekkanen, founding editor of New Orphic Review, for his early encouragement of early drafts of this novella and for his courageous support of struggling writers everywhere.

I thank my thoughtful readers: Kate Harkin, Margaret E. Ward, Nathaniel Foote, Mari Fitzduff, and Carol Wilson for their encouragement, insights, and critical commentaries.

I want to acknowledge Lisa Brennan for her artistic talent in crafting a fitting cover.

Finally, I want to thank Anne Racer, my wife and life long partner, for her indispensable editorial support, unflagging belief in the merits of my writing, and hilarious sense of humor when lightness of being was in short supply.

# About the Author

THOMAS RICE GREW UP IN County Carlow, Ireland, before emigrating first to Sheffield, England, then to New York, while still a teenager. He graduated from Cornell University and went on to a career as a professor and practitioner of sociology. To that end, in 1992 he co-founded the Interaction Institute for Social Change(IISC), focused on social justice. Since turning to fulltime writing in 2008, he has published several short stories, including "Border Calls," "All Souls' Day," and "The Night of the Arabian." In 2010 he published *Far From The Land*, a well-received memoir about growing up in Post WWII Ireland. In 2012, Robert Crais (as guest editor) selected one of his stories,"Hard Truths," for inclusion in *The Best American Mystery Stories of 2012*. He lives in Andover, Massachusetts, and Peaks Island, Maine.

**Cover design by Lisa Brennan**

www.ingramcontent.com/pod-product-compliance
Lightning Source LLC
Chambersburg PA
CBHW030631130626
46552CB00002B/802